MW00478801

WHY
WILLIE MAE
THORNTON
MATTERS

Music
Matters

Evelyn McDonnell and Oliver Wang

Series Editors

WHY WILLIE MAE THORNTON MATTERS

Lynnée Denise

UNIVERSITY OF TEXAS PRESS

AUSTIN

Requests for permission to reproduce material from this work should be sent to:
    Permissions
    University of Texas Press
    P.O. Box 7819
    Austin, TX 78713-7819
    utpress.utexas.edu

♾ The paper used in this book meets the minimum requirements of ANSI/NISO Z39.48-1992 (R1997) (Permanence of Paper).

Library of Congress Cataloging-in-Publication Data

Names: Denise, Lynnée (DJ), author.
Title: Why Willie Mae Thornton matters / Lynnée Denise.
Other titles: Music matters.
Description: First edition. | Austin : University of Texas Press, 2023. | Series: Music matters | Includes bibliographical references.
Identifiers: LCCN 2022055982 (print) | LCCN 2022055983 (ebook)
    ISBN 978-1-4773-2118-8 (hardcover)
    ISBN 978-1-4773-2794-4 (pdf)
    ISBN 978-1-4773-2795-1 (epub)
Subjects: LCSH: Thornton, Big Mama. | Thornton, Big Mama—Influence. | Women blues musicians—United States—Biography. | Black women singers—Biography. | Black women musicians—Biography. | Blues (Music)—History and criticism.
Classification: LCC ML420.T467 D45 2023 (print) | LCC ML420.T467 (ebook) | DDC 782.421643092 [B]—dc23/eng/20221123
LC record available at https://lccn.loc.gov/2022055982
LC ebook record available at https://lccn.loc.gov/2022055983

doi:10.7560/321188

The publication of this book was made possible by the generous support of the Brad and Michele Moore Roots Music Endowment.

This book is dedicated to my grandmother Dorothy Gathright (the first bluesy woman I ever met), bell hooks (an academic blueswoman), Toni Morrison, Zora Neale Hurston, Greg Tate, MF DOOM, Betty Carter, Roberta Flack, Winnie Mandela, Miriam Makeba, Busi Mhlongo, Alice Coltrane, Dorothy Ashby, Ruth Brown, Esther Phillips, Aretha Franklin, Louise Simone Bennett-Coverley (Miss Lou), Shug Avery, Sarah Vaughan, Claudia Jones, Cedella Marley, Abbey Lincoln, Lorraine Hansberry, Teena Marie, Ann Allen Shockley, Rosetta Tharpe, LaWanda Page, Pharoah Sanders, Phyllis Hyman, Moms Mabley, Latasha Harlins, and every ancestor who ghostwrote this book with me.

CONTENTS

INTRODUCTION

I started chasing Willie Mae "Big Mama" Thornton's story because of the biography I heard in her voice. My journey began when I watched her 1970 performance of "Ball 'n' Chain" with the Buddy Guy Blues Band. She walks onto the stage, nods to greet the band, and without saying a word scans the audience for nearly fifteen seconds before introducing the song. Some of that time is spent shaking her head, eyes closed, taking in the sound of Buddy's electric guitar. As she does this, the audience observes a private meditation on stage. Written all over Willie Mae's face during this performance, in between the scars her life had earned her, was an awareness of her power as a musician. She wore a two-piece denim suit with a fat, pointed collar. As far as fashion goes, this outfit was ahead of its time, giving her the androgynous look she fought to preserve throughout her career. On top of her head sat a crown—a solid black Cossack fur hat, calling to mind an African dignitary like Winnie Mandela. To complicate things, she wore rhinestone drop earrings. She appeared glassy-eyed and slightly buzzed, yet her skin was glowing and her words were clear. In this state she was on time and on beat—maybe numb from years of clarity about the cost of fame in an industry that systematically stole from Black artists. Willie Mae Thornton was a witness and a carrier of stories.

This movement I'm doing on the page is the literary embodiment of a specialized listening practice. I'm listening to her listen to musicians and shout out cues that swing between encouraging and reprimanding. I hear and see in Willie Mae the ways of infamous bandleaders like James Brown, Nina Simone, Lauryn Hill, and Prince, who weren't above docking pay or humiliating the band to achieve a superior sound with a sharp side-eye. Like the great blueswomen who came before and after her, Willie Mae was clear about what she wanted to achieve, and she was uncompromising if ever a note went astray. History treats women who know this pursuit of musical supremacy differently from men. Instead of being crowned geniuses, they get labeled demanding "divas." For this work, I decided to listen differently.

My experience of listening to Willie Mae Thornton's story is dependent on the set of ears I'm using to hear. As a DJ, I'm confronted by potential samples and other genres that can be mixed and blended with her style(s) of music. Second, I hear the difference between listening to her voice through a digital filter (CDs or MP3s) versus hearing it jump off a piece of vinyl—a format that captures finer details of the song's qualities—including the hisses and pops between music and lyrics. Third, I hear the evolution of her discography based on her relationships with record labels. Finally, I'm listening for the different places where she can be cataloged in my collection, and how she fits comfortably in categories like the one inspired by her unexpected excursion into the world of Haight Ashbury hippies—West Coast folk-blues—where Willie Mae makes sense next to Jose Feliciano, Richie Havens, Odetta, and Joan Armatrading. She, like the other artists of this ilk, forced preexisting notions of Blackness and music to take into consideration Black artist–led, cross-genre fusions. So perhaps the question I'm trying to answer in this book is what it means not only to listen to the sounds Willie Mae makes but also to hear the details of the life she crafted and lived.

In Willie Mae, I hear a philosopher who dropped out of elementary school. I hear a superb understanding of theory from a person who never learned to read or write music. In this, she reminds me of Jimi Hendrix, a fellow rhythm rebel who straddled genres because he bucked the restriction of formal training and because his hyper-intuitive musical literacy was coupled with discipline and skill. I hear Willie Mae's confidence and command of the stage as well as the matriarchal masculine force with which she holds this space across genres and decades. As the granddaughter of a Black woman from Mississippi, I hear in Willie Mae's music what I call sharecropper soul— of the field-hollering variety.

I think of Willie Mae holding the harmonica or playing the drums and I see her hands. Hands that tell the story of the part-time shoeshine business she set up in the front of venues where she performed in different cities during the first decade of her career. Hands that speak to the first job she held, cleaning the tobacco spittoons in a local saloon. Hands that convinced the saloon owner to allow her to replace the singer who was too drunk to perform. Hands that operated the garbage truck Willie Mae worked on at age fourteen, a job offered to her because she was taller than the average boy. Hands that caught the attention of Diamond Teeth Mary, who, according to Willie Mae's biographer, insisted that she get off that truck, "stop dressing like a boy," and audition for Sammy Green's Hot Harlem Revue in 1940. And with those hands, she earned a place in the revue and a pathway out of her widowed father's beloved Alabama. But still, Willie Mae, brilliantly stubborn, refused to stop "dressing like a boy." She instead wore a double-breasted suit throughout her career, including the last time she performed on stage forty years later.

The stylistic elements in Willie Mae's music were shaped by her eight-year stint with Sammy Green's Hot Harlem Revue. She also worked the Chitlin' Circuit, an underground network of events and venues that allowed Black artists who were excluded from white mainstream venues, to perform for their own communities in Black-owned clubs and makeshift spaces. Her experience in the 1940s revue and the 1950s Chitlin' Circuit scene is essential to understanding her as an artist. With Sammy Green's Hot Harlem Revue, she was professionally trained as an interdisciplinary artist, performing as a singer, dancer, and comedian who played the drums and harmonica while adhering to the regional styles demanded by audiences. In this way, she echoed the renaissance qualities of Chitlin' Circuit contemporaries like Little Richard and Moms Mabley, two crowd-pleasing queer artists with incredible showmanship, impeccable comedic timing, and larger-than-life personas.

No listening is complete without an ear tuned to her mastery of stage performance. A responsible Willie Mae listening practice means a commitment to seeing her perform live, even when there is little archival footage of her stage show available.

Promoters were so aware of her power as a live artist that they made sure to schedule her as the last performer on a bill. This was an act of mercy, for few artists could follow her. She was also one of a few women who performed the blues at state prisons, frequently singing love songs to the imprisoned male audience without bothering to change the pronouns from she to he.

Willie Mae's innovative, improvisational songwriting along with her theatrical performances landed her in Europe in 1965 and 1972 as the only woman selected to headline the American Folk Blues Festival. And it was at this festival, which traveled to cities such as Amsterdam, Berlin, and London, that she introduced Europeans to the "Down Home Shakedown," a song featuring a line of harmonica players: John Lee Hooker, Big Walter Horton, and Dr. Ross. Each blues giant watched for Willie Mae's approval and instruction during the performance, which she granted through head nods and a call-and-response, harmonica-based, syncopated groove. What we're talking about in the story of Willie Mae Thornton is the global reach of the Black South. Like Fannie Lou Hamer, she was a radical southerner.

Many residents in small southern towns like Ariton, Alabama, where Willie Mae was born, bought "race records" of early blues singers and developed their voices in the informal yet highly sophisticated musical training of the Black church. She wasn't exposed to country and vaudeville blues until she left home. "The only thing I heard locally was spirituals," she told producer Chris Strachwitz, "like quartets." Yet every song and performance I've discovered through my deep dive into her discography offers a story that unfolds into what I call blues ministry: an integrated sound made up of jook joint decadence and old-time religion. Willie Mae, the daughter of a minister and a mother she described as "Christian-hearted," made testifiers out of blues listeners. Blues ministry explains the centuries-old rift between spiritual and secular music. If the Black church was one of the first independent cultural institutions following the "emancipation" of formerly enslaved people, so too was the jook joint, where certain congregation members were as faithful to Saturday-night sinning as they were to Sunday-morning service. Blues ministry makes music out of the tension in these seemingly opposing forces; each note is a harmonious reckoning.

Willie Mae Thornton's musical range, gender-nonconforming politics, and multifaceted talent make it tricky to define both her role in the industry and her place in music history. In *Blues Legacies and Black Feminism*, which served as one of the guiding voices for this book, Angela Davis notes that Black women were the first to record the blues; in the 1920s "hundreds of women had the opportunity to record their work, even though they were systematically denied the financial benefits of their labor and the social benefits of recognition." This, too, is Willie Mae's story. But more significant than this shared experience of exploitation and erasure is the political footing on which many women stood. Davis suggests the blueswomen from the 1920s "divulged unacknowledged traditions of feminist consciousness in working-class black communities." This take on the blues gives me confidence to place her in a feminist blues tradition no matter where she fits on the music spectrum. Blues as ideology. Performance as resistance.

Willie Mae represents how musical cross-pollination was made possible through popular migration routes. One cannot discuss her legacy without mention of Mississippi

Delta blues, Chicago blues, Memphis soul, Houston rhythm and blues, Alabama gospel, California Central Avenue jazz, New York bebop, Bay Area psychedelic rock, and Pacific Northwest folk. Her footprint as an artist can be found all over the map, and pieces of her story appear in the liner notes of artists she collaborated with or influenced throughout her journey. Willie Mae also surfaces in the work of scholars of the blues, R&B, soul, feminism, and genderqueer studies. Still, she and others are mostly missing from conversations about how Black women artists helped build the foundation for the multibillion-dollar American popular music industry. So it must be stated with certainty that Willie Mae Thornton, like Rosetta Tharpe, Chuck Berry, and Muddy Waters, shares the bill with the architects of rock 'n' roll music. "Hound Dog," as famous as it is, was merely an inkling of what she offered American rock 'n' roll. Because this song and the story that surrounds it has been documented ad nauseam, I consciously sit with the stories on the edges of the song's history. Yes, I believe Elvis Presley recorded "Hound Dog" because he heard Willie Mae embody the song's sentiment with relentless conviction. Alice Walker shared a similar belief and used it as source material for her classic short story "Nineteen Fifty-Five." But in shifting the context of "Hound Dog" by writing in fiction form, Walker gave us the language to call Willie Mae by a new name, all the more important since naming for Black people is a contested site.

A key question that emerged when I began writing *Why Willie Mae Thornton Matters* is what name I would call her throughout the book. Born Minnie Willie Mae Thornton, she was given the stage name "Big Mama" by the white Apollo manager Frank Schiffman during a 1950s residency of hers at the historic theater. I had grown uncomfortable with the name upon reading encountering too often the writing of journalists, critics, and fellow musicians who refer to her as "Big Mama" in a way that seemed to reduce her massive artistic presence to her physical size. Calling her "Big Mama" got in the way of her being seen or discussed as a serious musician. My apprehension about the "Big Mama" part of her name exists in a world where Black women of a certain stature get caught up in a collective American imagination that reads them as asexualized matriarchs carrying the nation and its children on their breasts. This is not the mothering that comes to mind when I think of the many Black women who collapsed or died while performing on stage or shortly thereafter (a list that includes Mahalia Jackson, Ella Fitzgerald, Tammi Terrell, and Miriam Makeba). Too many of our aunties and Big Mamas have lived and died on stage, and for too long they carried the weight of white America through song.

The answer to the question of her name became clear upon watching footage of an interview with Ray Charles. When asked about Elvis, Charles broke down his frustration with Presley's ascendance. He cited the reasons for his disapproval of the word "king" to describe Presley: "He was doing our kind of music. He was doing the Willie Mae Thornton . . . that's Black music, so what the hell am I supposed to get so excited about, man?" It was in that moment that I realized Ray Charles had removed "Big Mama" and put the word "the" in front of Willie Mae's name, as if she were a dance craze circulating in a secret society where only insiders had access to the coded movement. In this universe Elvis was denied entry. I call her Willie Mae throughout the book because of what I felt when Ray Charles called her Willie Mae. I wrote this book because in the name Willie Mae Thornton is the sound of Black musical resilience.

When I searched for more clues about Willie Mae's story I discovered that not a single American had written her biography. A full interrogation of her meaning to the world of music has only been done once before. That's how I ended up in Düsseldorf, Germany, in the summer of 2018, to meet the lone biographer of Willie Mae Thornton, Michael Spörke. Michael was generous from our first email interaction and welcomed my visit with the promise of an interview and a peek at his sources. Michael managed to find friends, family, and colleagues of Willie Mae's who understood the value of oral history and the art of animated storytelling. In our interview, he spoke extensively about wanting to clear Willie Mae's name. He felt that stories that still circulated in the industry painted her as a mean, violent drunk instead of an assertive and unfeminine woman who questioned the business practices of the men whom she trusted with her career. Her politics of refusal had everything to do with the integrity in her sound, and he knew this. She refused to be quiet when her money was on the line, refused to wear a dress as she was expected to, and refused to sing songs the way producers envisioned them.

He also wanted to put to rest the rumors surrounding her sexuality. Throughout his book, he references how often people within her circle stated emphatically that Willie Mae was a lesbian. Spörke, with great passion, lamented that they never provided evidence for this assertion. It was as though he was protecting her from the mere possibility of being queer, and therefore missed an opportunity to add a more layered story about her life. *Why Willie Mae Thornton Matters* is not invested in filing her under the Black blues lesbian category. Instead, through the careful examination of her music, I would like to make space for her to exist on the spectrum of sexuality without having either one of us lay claim to a singular sexual identity. Maybe the most radical thing Willie Mae left behind is that she did not identify as queer or butch or lesbian or gay — at least not publicly. My sense is that she didn't hate wearing dresses; she loved wearing pants. Willie Mae always carried a harmonica on her; dresses provided fewer options to store her tools.

Writing this book as a Californian Black queer woman who grew up in the 1980s hip-hop era allows for a unique telling of her journey. I am committed to adding a nuanced read on Willie Mae Thornton that is more humanizing and less cis-heteronormative than what has come before. To share why she matters is to build on Spörke's work and offer to her life a new level of intimacy, one that comes from a sense of fictive kinship — me as the long-lost niece with familial knowing. And as her niece I experienced days when I felt like Willie Mae called me to be a voice on her life's page. On some days I felt chosen and equipped; on other days, overwhelmed and irresponsible. Who was I to step into her world and piece together a cohesive literary survey on her movement through Black music? How could this be done with the one biography that existed and the fragmented history I was left to decipher? Finally, the answer became clear. It was my job as a Black queer DJ and scholar to approach this biography as I would a mixtape. Willie Mae's story, in my hands, emerges from the mixtape process.

Mixtapes tell the story of your skills; they function like an archive of the community's musical tastes as shaped by DJs. Adam Banks describes the DJ as one who is "standing between tradition and future, holding the power to shape how both are seen/heard/felt/known. Exhibiting mastery of techniques, but always knowing that techniques carry stories, arguments, ways of viewing the world, that the techniques arrange the texts, that every text carries even more stories, arguments, epistemologies." My relationship with the needle, and what happens when it's dropped on a piece of vinyl, is what taught me how to write this book. The Willie Mae literary mixtape results from years spent determining the value of songs, reading and writing liner notes, studying album cover art, chasing samples, digging through the crates, and — like the Zulu Nation — "looking for the perfect beat," but also "lookin' searchin' seekin' and findin'" the metaphoric unmarked graves of women musicians, producers, and performers who helped develop my ear. This is DJ scholarship, a term I coined in 2013 to introduce to the culture a methodological intervention.

So yes, my job is to remember and remake the story, even if that story is a collection of small parts that compose the whole. A mixtape is, after all, a sound collage of found objects, people, places, and concepts used to create a composition. That said, I admit, there are times when you will read this Willie Mae story and get lost until you catch the beat. This is not your typical biography. This journey into Willie Mae's life reads more like a biography in essays. I appear in some chapters using personal experiences and memories to get close to Willie Mae's sound. In other chapters I disappear altogether to let her journey take center stage. There are unexpected comparisons between Willie Mae and artists like Roxanne Shanté and connections made between Texas R&B and Jamaican ska.

The record of Willie Mae's absence from the annals of music history speaks to an ongoing politic of erasure of Black women cultural producers, in both the music industry and American society at large. Because of the generation she belonged to, we've run out of time to survey and secure accounts of her greatness and artistry from living witnesses. Very few of her contemporaries are still with us. Now is the time to create a mixtape for why she matters. I believe she died knowing what she did, for America, for Black music, and that brings me the most comfort when sitting with her archive. I hope to fill the gaps in her story with a politic of care. To blend, as a DJ would, her life of touching histories. Her righteous anger motivates me, especially the cases in which she transforms it into a playful threat and a sound cloud to which we are invited to look up and stand under. This book is a love letter from one difficult woman to another.

MOTHERING THE BLUES

Mother is the single most interesting and confusing word that I know. Next to Black.

ALEXIS PAULINE GUMBS

I once had a play mama. She was older, popular, and adept
at braiding and tidying up the girls—her girls—on the
yard. I was chosen to be one of her daughters because I
could dance. The timing of my invitation to be part of
this middle school chosen family was perfect. It was 1987,
and my mother, like many mothers on that LA block, was
under the spell of addiction. I knew her mothering was
on the line when the tender moment of doing my hair for
school pictures escaped possibility. That moment when,
sitting between her legs as she parted—starting from the
tip of my nose to the hairline—had come and gone. When
picture day arrived, we both knew, Mom and I, that she
would not be leaving her bed and that I was on my own
for this annual celebration. And when I arrived at school
that morning, early enough for free breakfast, my play
mama glanced at my hair and stepped in. Always prepared, she had rubber bands, decorative balls, and a comb
with a fishtail end. She weaved her way through the breakfast crowd, found a table, sat me down on the bench, and

started parting—from the tip of my nose—as I sat quietly between her legs.

Back at home, the music played on. No matter what condition my mother's heart was in, she played her music so loud I could recognize certain tunes as I approached our street. Her withdrawal process was a reckoning that had a soundtrack, and it was through her mothering, even if from her grief bed, that I learned that the women she listened to—Ella, Gladys, Patti—were mothering her too. The truth is, when she felt drowned by her battle, my mother returned to the womb—which was the same color as the blues and just the way Lady Day sang them.

In the anthology *Revolutionary Mothering: Love on the Front Lines*, Alexis Pauline Gumbs calls for other ways of being and existing in motherhood. She offers an expansive framing of Black people who mother and invites us to consider mothering not as a patriarchal, heteronormative reading of cis women and biological birthing, but as a liberating queer act beyond gender binaries. In the anthology's introduction, Gumbs explains that "many people do the labor of mothering who would never even dream of identifying as mothers, even though they do the daily intergenerational care work of making a hostile world an affirming space for another person who is growing mentally, spiritually, physically, and emotionally." This world of motherhood inspired a reimagining of queen mothers in the ballroom scene, the mothering of organizations and social movements, the mothering of theory and praxis, and, in Willie Mae Thornton's case, a butch-femme mothering of the blues. I am grateful for this queering of motherhood; it's allowed me to listen differently to songs that rendered me a child who was motherless. Both my mother and my play mama are still here, still mothering people, places, and ideas, and I'm still here, tickled by the spectrum of mothering that makes motherlessness an impossibility.

Winnie Willie Mae Thornton was born on December 11, 1926. Her mother, Mattie Haynes, was born in 1893 and led the choir as a singer in George W. Thornton's Baptist church. George, born in 1876, was Willie Mae's father. Mattie and George had six children, three sons (Judge, C. W., and George, Jr.) and three daughters (Gussie, Roxie, and Willie Mae). In 1928 Mattie Haynes lost one child, E. W., within one year of giving birth. George Thornton had another child outside the marriage, Willie Mae's half sister Mattie Fields, who remained a crucial part of her life from the time they attended a one-room school together in Alabama in the 1930s, until the last days of Willie Mae's life when she was said to have called Mattie to say goodnight for a final time before her 1984 death in California. Willie Mae's maternal grandparents, Caleb Haynes, Sr., and Eliza Jones, were born into slavery and had twelve children — five girls and seven boys. Her introduction to how family structures functioned like social networks that pooled resources became evident when she dropped out of school at age twelve in 1938 to care for her sick mother, a forced decision that left her functionally illiterate and vulnerable to predatorial music industry practices.

When Willie Mae left Alabama as a teenager, shortly following her mother's 1939 death from tuberculosis in a Montgomery sanatorium, she was mothered by performers in the entertainment industry — vaudeville women who introduced her to the blues and the business. I have a duty to make this mothering clear. It is not possible to write about Willie Mae without drawing on the work of people I hold to be Black mothers and daughters of blues scholarship and Black women who mothered Willie Mae throughout her journey.

One thing that hangs around my childhood memory is traveling to Rush City in East St. Louis during summers and discovering the single gold tooth worn by the women on my father's side of the family. I found later that gold teeth behind Black lips were common on the continent of Africa and a shared practice among Black and Brown people globally, "From South Africa to South Carolina," as Gil Scott Heron titled his 1975 LP. Many theories try to explain this cultural protocol, one being that gold teeth represented a kind of regality that outshone the social conditions that would have you think otherwise about the resources we possessed. One could have a gold tooth and share a two-room shack with three people, and onlookers, greeted by the glow from your mouth, would be forced to recognize how Black people embodied wealth beyond its material availability. That's why Diamond Teeth Mary stands out to me. Like my grandmother's sisters, she adorned her body with fancy jewels and stones. After years of touring with various medicine and minstrel shows in the 1920s and 1930s, she found the kind of financial security that allowed her to buy diamond bracelets and necklaces. Embodying what would later be described as bling, Mary removed $5,000 worth of the diamonds from her jewelry and had them set into her upper and lower front teeth. Forty years later, the Slauson Swapmeet provided these same services for Black people in the Crenshaw area in Los Angeles. Inside the Swapmeet's bright green building was an abundance of options, including engraved lettering, gold fronts, and open-face triples. And it does something to me to know that Ma Rainey, Koko Taylor, Sippie Wallace, MC Lyte, and my great aunt Mae-Lou rocked some variation of mouth gold too. Diamond Mary was a trendsetter and went to great lengths to communicate that she knew her value, which means that gold fronts are political, even beyond the political nature of how gold from Africa finds its way to the States and the Swapmeet in the first place. Diamond Mary was working for Sammy Green's Hot Harlem Revue when she encountered a young Willie Mae. The revue was touring the South when Mary heard a big voice coming from a small child. Willie Mae was only fourteen when Diamond Mary encouraged her to audition for Sammy, and she wooed the judges that day in 1940 and secured a spot soon after. Diamond Mary stepped into the role of play mama for Willie Mae.

I'm not sure when the word "play" used to describe unrelated family members entered my lexicon but having play mamas and play cousins — play family in general — gave me confidence as a preteen growing up in Los Angeles. Play mamas and play cousins were my introduction to the boundless world of chosen family. Later in life, as a DJ and a student of Black queer cultural production, I got hip to the fact that house mothers and house fathers were thought leaders in queer survival strategies. The ballroom culture formed in New York in the '80s, which hit the mainstream through the documentary *Paris Is Burning*, was full of play mamas and play fathers. They were recognized as people who protected the young from toxic family dynamics and antigay violence. Chosen family structures were also a response to the people who were disappeared by mass incarceration, the War on Drugs, and other hostile Reagan policies. The truth is, a lot of us lost and gained mothers in the '80s. Abolitionists such as Angela Davis and Ruthie Wilson Gilmore determined through extensive scholarship that when Black women go to prison, it's the maternal grandmothers, aunts, and older sisters who most often step in. This means that at the core of play families are subversive queer reunions. In this case, Willie Mae carrying the title "Big Mama" is a standard Black queer intervention.

Given her unique position in the blues and her performance antics, I understand why on many occasions throughout her six studio and two live albums Willie Mae refers to herself in third person as "Big Mama." She embraced and even weaponized the "Big Mama" title when she needed to get the point across. "Come here closer, so Big Mama can hit you with a brick," she tells a sly suitor in the song "Three O'Clock Blues." Her third-person play also gives her the space she needs to exist offstage; Big Mama is, in fact, her narrator, the protagonist in her animated blues tales. I get the feeling that Willie Mae was part of Big Mama's audience. The unique and historical use of the term "Big Momma" in Black communities is more intriguing, as is how Willie Mae complicates and complements its meaning. "Big Momma," Black Detroit linguist Geneva Smitherman says, refers to the Black grandmother as a central figure in the Black family household who keeps the kids while the parents work: "Though white sociology has depicted Big Momma as a big-bosomed emasculating matriarch, she was, in fact, the anchor and core that held the family together through her unselfish sacrifice and warm love that nurtured her grandchildren through the storm and taught them to keep their 'eye on the sparrow.'" Willie Mae's third-person use of "Big Mama" accepts the role of care for her audiences and listeners (the proverbial grandchildren) through storytelling — and sometimes the care shifts from the grandchildren to Big Mama's care of her own heart.

Willie Mae also sees herself as a figure with unyielding authority who will hurt you if necessary. In the hands of Willie Mae, Big Mama is also a teacher of Black blues humor. She not only escapes the white sociological gaze but centers Black privacy by speaking in code. The Black English she speaks only reaches those who read, live, and understand it. Willie Mae's Big Mama is not concerned with emasculating men. Her appearance and ad-libs insist that she *is* the masculine matriarch, and one should do what it takes to avoid double-crossing Big Mama if a rock is near.

In the song "They Call Me Big Mama," recorded by Peacock Records in the early '50s, Willie Mae connects her name to her size: "Well they call me Big Mama / 'Cause I weigh three hundred pounds." However, her public discussion of weight is less about self-degradation, a poor self-image, and the hostility attached to the way fat and bigger-bodied people (particularly Black women) have been ridiculed in America for centuries. Instead, her three hundred pounds are a source of pride and power. The weight of both her body and her words offer a complex mix of protection.

In their essay "Queer Voices, Musical Genders," Jack Halberstam posed a question about gender, sex, and blues complexity: "Why are so many blueswomen cast as 'ma' or 'mama'? What dramas of production and reproduction are set in motion by the apparent clash between female masculinity and the maternal?" Halberstam continues, "The terms 'mama' and 'daddy,' were and are used in African-American vernacular to express lover relationships as much as familial relations and in some blues lyrics, 'daddy' could as easily refer to a butch female lover as to a male lover. The unmooring of parental labels from the function of parenting itself and the tethering of these terms to sexual roles implies that the domestic has been queered." I've embraced the maternal references used to describe women in the blues, and I love wrestling with the contradictions, conflicts, and plot twists built within them. However, it gets complicated when considering the place Black women have occupied in the American imagination as the ever-present, apolitical, asexualized mammy or matriarch. As Hortense Spillers points out in her essay "Interstices: A Small Drama of Words," "The beached whales of the sexual universe, unvoiced, misseen, not doing, *awaiting* their verb." But I can easily see a Black lover instigating a flirtatious encounter with Willie Mae by calling her — while she dons a three-piece suit made for the bodies of cis men — Big Mama or Daddy.

The counter-maternal narrative produced by some early blueswomen is an essential point of interest for me. Beyond the mother/father blues binary, I'm interested in the kind of bodies that share the margins with blueswomen — queer, gender-nonconforming, and trans folk included. The first recorded blueswomen spoke openly about their sexual fluidity and pushed up against gender norms. Willie Mae's recalcitrant fashion choices, the way she strutted in them cowboy boots and her Texas wide-brimmed hat, forced a new spelling of blues femininity and, eventually, a new spelling of blues, funk, and soul masculinity too.

In her book *Cultures in Babylon*, Hazel Carby points to the typical physical appearance of those who would be called blueswomen in the early twentieth century, noting that they "occupied a privileged space; they had broken out of the boundaries of the home and taken their sensuality and sexuality out of the private into the public sphere. . . . Their physical presence was a crucial aspect of their power; their visual display of spangled dresses, of furs, of gold teeth, of diamonds, of all the sumptuous and desirable aspects of their body, reclaimed female sexuality from being an objectivization of male desire to a representation of female desire." While Carby's observations are accurate, I wonder how many women in the industry were erased or disappeared if they didn't embrace the widely accepted, though subversive, fashion choices of earlier blueswomen? Where do we place Willie Mae generationally in a description and discussion of gender, blues, and fashion? Is she the spiritual daughter of Gladys Bentley or Moms Mabley? How do we understand the furless, dressless performer who was unconventionally desirable and more aligned, in appearance, with bluesmen?

Another thing that surfaced in my research on Willie Mae is the reluctance, by journalists and critics who attempt to describe her play with gender, to call her sexy. For me, calling a masculine cis woman sexy is one way of reclaiming or resituating the use of "sexy" as a gendered term typically reserved for cis men and femmes. Her decision to free herself from gender norms challenges students of her work and life to move away from the unimaginative adjectives that limit descriptions of Willie Mae to her height and weight. What else about her person can we highlight? I acknowledge that "sexy" and "beautiful" can be both problematic and subjective words. But I see Willie Mae Thornton as a sexy woman, and I pay close attention to both the defiance that shaped the sound of her voice and her decision to buck gender rules at a time when that could cost you your career. Willie Mae understood her erotic magic, her sensual power — the legible energy that materialized in her music. My feeling is that because Willie Mae never "came out" or disclosed her sexuality, she's become vulnerable to the erasure of her sexuality altogether. She was incredibly private about whom she loved, but I do not believe in "playing it safe" by using heterosexuality as a default descriptor until the historical record proves otherwise. I do not know if Willie Mae Thornton identified as lesbian, but she was gender nonconforming, which, by definition, is queer.

What I'm speaking to here is Spillers's charge that Black women's sexuality has been "unvoiced, misseen." We don't need to know whom Willie Mae slept with and whom she loved romantically to acknowledge her sex appeal. And some of us can admit that her play with gender performance drove fans, listeners, and audiences to wonder who Wille Mae was speaking to when wrapped up in a traditional, seductive blues ballad. Who is Willie Mae's narrator speaking to in the song "Sweet Little Angel" when she insists that listeners take pity on the fact that "when my baby quit me, I believed I would die"? She found a home in the anonymity the blues provides. The blues found a home in Willie Mae as well.

In an interview with the writer Studs Terkel, Willie Mae Thornton spoke about the first time she experienced the blues: "I really got the blues in 1939 when I lost my mother and then I said, 'I don't know what to do, but I think I want to sing the blues.' I was listening to Big Maceo's 'Worried Life Blues' and said, 'I think I want to sang that.'" Willie Mae auditioned the song for Sammy Green's Hot Harlem Revue and later described for Terkel with amusement what she wore on the day her life changed: "I had on a pair of jeans, one leg rolled up and I got up and I started singing Louis Jordan's song called 'GI Jive,' and I sang that song and Big Maceo's 'Worried Life Blues,' and he hired me. Out of twenty-five people, I was number twenty-six and he hired me." I love this story because there's a discrepancy in her timeline, which makes me think about Black people and our unpredictable dance with memory. We have every right to reshape our stories, considering the wildly unreasonable life circumstances we've known for centuries. Amiri Baraka refers to the blues itself as a form of "racial memory." What's interesting in Willie Mae's story, though, is that "GI Jive" was written in 1944, four years *after* Willie Mae auditioned at the Pekin Theatre in Montgomery. I think of this play with blues racial memory as autobiographical fiction and place it next to Audre Lorde's "biomythography."

"GI Jive" was an advanced number for Willie Mae Thornton, a fourteen- or eighteen-year-old who, according to her re-memory, sang it as part of her first audition. Regardless of the rhetorical devices needed to perform Jordan's version, Willie Mae had to make a living. She entered the entertainment world with a blues-heavy heart from the loss of her mother and learned early that pushing yourself was something you had to do. You had to excel in the craft to secure food, clothing, and shelter, even if you were fourteen. According to Willie Mae, "GI Jive" was one of the songs that gave birth to her body of work. With this song, she became a mother of her own blues; moreover, around the same time, she became a mother of her own child.

Upon reading the last sentences in the opening chapter of Michael Spörke's biography, I was saddened and shattered. Discussing the early part of her life on the road with Sammy Green's Hot Harlem Revue, he says, "If it wasn't hard enough for a young girl, Willie Mae became pregnant about this time and had a son. She kept the son with her on the road and tried to be a good mother, but the authorities took her boy away from her. Willie Mae Thornton would only rarely talk about that later, but it must have left a big hole in her heart." There are no footnotes, no further explanations, no subsequent chapters that pick up from where that chapter ends. All we're left with is the big hole in Willie Mae's heart and the child who was taken away from her. There is no rationale for why Spörke feels like "she tried to be a good mother" and no insight about what it means to be a "good" mother at fourteen years old. I feel uneasy about his handling of this moment because I want more for Willie Mae as a mother.

I want this gap in her story to make us think about her as more than an unlucky musician followed by a string of unfortunate events. That's why I started reflecting on the high maternal and infant mortality rates of Black women. And the number of children born in prison to shackled Black mothers. And the number of Black children swallowed by the foster care system. I wondered what it must have felt like to be Fannie Lou Hamer and the thousands of nameless Black women who were sterilized without permission. Reading while Black requires caution and vigilance. It's a world where land mines are disguised as sentences. I had no idea how to hold this information and what to make of the big hole in her heart. Did it show up in her music? Was the hole filled with gin? How old was the father of the child? Was the sex consensual? What happened to Willie Mae's son? Is he still with us? Does he remember her voice? I've spent time looking for Willie Mae's nameless child, and I'm sure that he, at some point in his life, was rendered motherless. The most important thing I can offer him, though, is the knowledge that he belonged to a Big Mama and, therefore, motherlessness is an impossibility.

THE BLACK SOUTH MATTERS

Both the black church and the blues emerged in rural areas where Black political and economic institutions were subjected to constant surveillance and often destroyed. Both prospered in Southern cities and spread throughout the Northern and Western Diasporas.

CLYDE WOODS

I believe in the fantastical possibility of being born again and being dead again. That's why I love Sun Ra and how he taught me that Alabama is a portal, a state that is not so much his place of birth, as much as it's where he first appeared. The body he used came to shape in Birmingham, and he took his last breath there, proving the logic in Zandria Robinson's and Marcus Hunter's *Chocolate Cities* that "Black life in modernity is a boomerang rather than a straight line of progress." But what Sun Ra has shown us is that Alabama is not only one of the most critical places to return to when undertaking Black music studies but also a place that offers a pathway to Saturn. We owe Alabama much more than repackaging abolitionist-sponsored, widely distributed generic slave narratives and gratuitous lynching stories. It's better to think of Alabama as a place where Black soul has, historically, driven white people to insanity, and there's a record of them taking aim at us for reasons that seem connected to our relationship with rhythm. For example, the Alabama Slave Laws of 1852 were less about Black rebellion and more a document of codified white fear. One such law could be found in section 17 of *A Digest of the Laws of the State of Alabama*: "It shall not be lawful for more than five male slaves, either with or without passes, to assemble together at any place off the proper plantation to which they belong. And if any slaves do so assemble together, the same shall be deemed an unlawful assembly." They created laws around the things that made us most human — the ability to come together to sing, dance, worship, love, and move freely. They feared Black folk with access to their full humanity, which could lead to a reversal of the fortune they found in Black labor. Whiteness is the science of insecurity, and Alabama Blackness deserves our attention.

It makes perfect sense that W. C. Handy, the self-proclaimed "father of the blues," is a son of Florence, Alabama. Despite her association with the Black Floridian town of Eatonville, anthropologist and blues scholar Zora Neale Hurston was born in Notasulga, Alabama. Likewise, it doesn't surprise me that Lula Mae Hardaway was born on a sharecropper's farm in Eufaula, Alabama, before she migrated to Michigan. Or that Lulu had a wonderful child named Stevland Morris, whom listeners of his music refer to as affectionately as Stevie. Or that the matriarch Katherine Jackson, born in Clayton, Alabama, moved to Indiana and gave birth to eight children, among them a shy one who wore white glittered socks and walked backward on the moon. The musical genius in Alabama soil is undeniable, and the slave laws (and adaptations of them into post-slavery statutes) were needed by whites to contain it.

To be honest, I haven't always felt this way. California is a place where, for as long as I can remember, good weed was abundant. In the 1980s, one's reputation could be tarnished by any attempt to smoke or sell what we, disrespectfully, called Bama weed. Bama was short for Alabama, and it implied that something was backward, old-fashioned, or inferior. When cousins came to visit from the South, we'd turn our noses up because the words they used hung in the air long after they finished speaking. Southern drawl, to us, sounded like the time before Black History Month was made official or King had a holiday. It didn't dawn on us that when we closed our eyes and listened to Cali rappers, which is to say, ourselves, we heard similar elements of that slow flow. It took moving to the South and falling in love with how Black people changed their cultural practices and fashion choices four times a year with the seasons to do it for me. It was seeing the reaction of friends and family when I told them I was leaving Los Angeles for Fisk University in Nashville to learn both how long we've employed these technologies of shaming Southerners and my role in it. But Zora Neale Hurston, consistent with her Capricornistic worldview and her Alabama roots, refused to give a damn. Withstanding alienation from several writers and artists from the Harlem Renaissance crew who called her out for uplifting all things "lowbrow," she took that Southern drawl and placed it alongside the folk languages of Jamaica and Haiti and built stories around the creolization of English. She taught us that Black folk in Haiti and Jamaica had their own languages, which were worthy of study too. She studied and used the blues, also considered lowbrow art by new Negro Renaissance migrants, as a composition to score the language of Black life. Zora Neale gave me the tools to understand Willie Mae Thornton beyond fragile state lines and false divisions.

Willie Mae Thornton was born on one of the funkiest pieces of land on earth. When asked about her birthplace by her former producer Chris Strachwitz, she, without hesitation, stated, "I'm an Alabama kid, Montgomery." Willie Mae's birth certificate places her birth in Ariton, Alabama. Dale County, to be exact. In *Chocolate Cities*, Hunter and Robinson speak to the long history of how people like Willie Mae answered questions about where they were born. In doing so, they dispel the myth that all Black migrants moved from the South to the North: "They left the plantations and rural towns of the South for the urban South, moving up to the nearest big Southern city. They left smaller Southern cities for bigger Southern cities. And they left Southern cities for large urban and near-urban areas of the eastern seaboard, the Midwest, the West, and stops in between." Willie Mae identified her place of birth as one of the most recognized Alabama chocolate cities instead of the lesser-known Ariton. The answer she gave reveals a larger story about Black geographies. The truth is, Willie Mae lived all over Alabama, like how my grandmother lived all over Mississippi and how my mother lived all over California. This phenomenon was especially common with Black families between the Reconstruction era and the Great Depression. Their movement patterns were determined by opportunity, love, and safety. Willie Mae's family left Ariton when she was a young child and moved to Troy City in Pike County. When her mother died, Willie Mae, alone, moved several miles east to live with relatives in Barbour County. She moved again and found domestic work and odd jobs as a teenager in Montgomery.

It's fair to say that Montgomery represents a birthplace of sorts for Willie Mae. That's where she got her big break and set out on a forty-year local, national, and world tour. On that tour she entered an extensive network of chosen family—a network of play mamas, play brothers, and play cousins. Willie Mae Thornton traveled to or made her home in various chocolate cities. With each stop, she picked up local secrets from fellow musicians and left for the next town with a more layered sound. Mark Anthony Neal points to how rhythms were passed from city to city, an essential trait of the traveling blues: "Popular performers at rent parties or in other leisure spaces were valued for their ability to conflate various regional styles, in effect creating a sound that would resonate across the [black American] diaspora. In this regard, the development of the urban blues contributed to the emergence of the black popular music tradition of the twentieth century." Willie Mae's childhood relationship to music occurred within the confines of the church, but her true baptism in Black popular music came from her Alabaman base and her pan-southern movement.

Willie Mae spent her first thirteen years in Alabama. Unlike performers such as Sam Cooke, Nina Simone, and Aretha Franklin (all children of ministers), she did not play a pivotal role in the church her father ministered or participate in any other formal singing. She had no relationship with popular music until she left home. Her musical roots in Alabama are steeped in the culture of the field hollers that were part of the soundscape of the plantations, chain gangs, and sharecropping operations that were still active as she moved throughout the state between 1926 and 1940. Upon leaving Alabama, Wille Mae settled in Atlanta between 1940 and 1948. For most of those years she was on the road, listening to and studying the South. She was also being listened to and studied by people in the South—a kind of rhythmic reciprocity. Recalling her first tour with Sammy Green, Willie Mae says to Chris Strachwitz, "We played in Atlanta, Birmingham, back home in Montgomery, Columbus, South Carolina, Florida. We played all over the South. When the war began, we played especially in theaters in Texas." She absorbed elements of Black performance practices, spun them to her liking, and tailored the sounds to fit her musical personality. This idea of a musical personality, and the magnetic power of it, was modeled by a young man who she met along the pan-southern way, a colorful character by the name of Richard Penniman.

Little Richard was punished by his father for being too close to his sisters and the local girls; he was seen as the "weakest link" among his brothers. Growing up he was very close to his mother, and later on he even shared with her the coded gay vernacular he picked up while traveling through the South. Mama, he'd say, "they call everybody Miss Thing." Decades later, when asked in a 1986 interview with Bill Boggs about his influences, Richard answered emphatically, "Mahalia Jackson, the Clara Ward Singers, and Ruth Brown." There is no doubt that Little Richard's Black femme divinity was well-informed. A different iteration of that femininity prompted another shift in his perspective and presentation when, touring through Georgia, he met Prince of the Blues Billy Wright. "Billy Wright," Richard said in his authorized biography, "was an entertainer that wore very loud-colored clothing, and he wore his hair curled. He influenced me a lot. He really enthused my whole life." Wright, Richard believed, was never given his due props for influencing generations of artists. Speaking to Wright's under-explored legacy, Richard said, "Outside a small circle, his importance has never been recognized, and his name is unknown. . . . He was a fantastic entertainer. His makeup was really something. I found out what it was and started using it myself. It was called Pancake 31." He also praised Billy Wright for inspiring him to wear his pompadour.

Willie Mae Thornton was one of the artists among the "small circle" who knew Billy Wright. She worked closely with him when he danced for Sammy Green's Revue and later when he signed to Peacock Records. She also ran some of the same streets as Little Richard in the late 1940s. The 81 Bailey Theater and the Auburn Avenue Royal Peacock scene in Atlanta were their shared landing spots. At fourteen Little Richard, a southerner raised in the church too, left home for the entertainment world. He was six years younger than Thornton.

Little Richard, Billy Wright, and Willie Mae Thornton, among others, provide an opportunity to queer the Chitlin' Circuit and the roots of R&B. These artists infused their radical gender performances and nonconventional gender expressions into the venues where they performed and the very genre itself. Still, the Chitlin' Circuit gets read as a cis Black straight project, with Little Richard and Willie Mae discussed as outliers. In reality, they belong to a massive collective of artists and trendsetters (primarily from the South) who rejected the framework of Black heteronormative cultural production while working around the construct of respectability politics and Black church judgment. I know identity is complicated. I always return to the fact that Willie Mae never declared or discussed her sexuality, so by "queer" I am denoting the spectrum of queerness and the diversity of sexual politics in Black communities across America. In the spirit of Judith Butler, I am thinking about a queerness that can refer to gender performance and doesn't stop or begin at sexual desire and sexual practice.

In her essay "Big Mama Thornton, Little Richard, and the Queer Roots of Rock 'n' Roll," historian Tyina Steptoe included a photograph of her grandfather Andrew Steptoe and Willie Mae Thornton in Houston. Both are wearing harem-style balloon pants and a white button-up shirt. Willie Mae, for extra flare, is sporting a dark, mid-length tie. Some folks might have labeled them "sissies" and "bulldaggers," terms that typically referred to gender presentation before World War II; some observers would have interpreted Thornton and Little Richard's gender nonconformity after the war as a sign of homosexuality. Steptoe notes how significant these shifts and meetings were for queer culture: "By joining traveling acts, or even attending their shows when these troupes came into town, queer people from small southern locales like Ariton, Alabama, or Macon, Georgia, encountered one another." That doesn't mean they could be open without fear of professional or personal retaliation. On the contrary, Steptoe continues, "Thornton and Penniman faced a different sociopolitical climate by the early fifties, which affected the ways queer themes could be presented in popular music. By the time they began recording, mass-produced and mass-distributed rhythm and blues, music did not contain the openly frank expressions of queer behavior found in classic blues records."

Little Richard, Willie Mae, and Billy Wright would each eventually sign with Peacock Records in the 1950s. As part of the Peacock package shows, Billy Wright and Willie Mae toured together with their labelmates. Package shows, like Motown's Motortown Revue that toured the country a decade later, allowed labels both to push their roster of artists without the costs of individual tours and to build trust around the uniformity offered by their brand. Following the success of "Hound Dog" in 1953, Willie Mae was added to the Peacock Blues Consolidated Package Show with Johnny Ace, Junior Parker, and Bobby "Blue" Bland. The lineup would change according to city and chart success. Package shows were typical of all tours for Black performers in that there was plenty of liquor, tons of sex, and riotous pleasure coupled with segregated hotels, hostile cops, and shady promoters. Rivalries and egos made for excellent performances as battles and beefs between artists fueled the crowd. Willie Mae's orchestrated rivalry with labelmate Marie Adams was a favorite for national audiences, and Willie Mae's added sense of humor left her opponent humiliated. She would turn her back while Adams performed or find another way to distract the crowd—vaudeville tactics that remained entertaining for a new generation.

There are more names to learn, but Willie Mae and Little Richard give us the compass we need to rediscover all the Black queer talent that crisscrossed the Southland. The South has always had something to say. Billy Wright, Moms Mabley, Rosetta Tharpe, Gladys Bentley, and Esquerita were among those who mothered Willie Mae and Little Richard in the Black South. This makes me think about how it takes discipline to do away with preconceived notions about the South and how the Black South gets sold as a monolith. I like to think of each southern state as a small country, and the region as a Black music motherland. Willie Mae and Little Richard show us that the motherland carries the stories of all the children, even the ones called freaks or Miss Thing.

SISTERS OF THE DIRTY BLUES

Yeah, Celie. Everything wanna be loved. Us sing and dance, and holla just wanting to be loved. Look at them trees. Notice how the trees do everything people do to get attention . . . except walk?

SHUG AVERY

I am her friend, and her tongue is in my mouth. I can speak her sentiments for her, though Ethel Waters can do very well indeed in speaking for herself.

ZORA NEALE HURSTON

The dirty blues was a subgenre of the blues typically performed by women who were artfully explicit in their ongoing missions to have every sexual desire fulfilled (by men or women) and would call you out if you came up short on the job. Reframing "dirty blues" as a metaphor for the music business helped me understand blueswomen networks and Willie Mae's role in them. Countless artists were exploited in the blues business (and the music business in general), including Willie Mae.

Referencing the work it took Ma Rainey and Bessie Smith to bring a show to the stage, Angela Davis writes about the administrative details of the traveling blues. These two women were "booking their shows, paying their musicians and dancers, and transporting them from city-to-city week after week and month after month." What were the collective survival strategies of less prominent blueswomen? Who were the women who introduced Willie Mae to the business—organizing her shows, coordinating her lodging, and securing her food? How did Willie Mae Thornton enter the industry as a teenage girl from Alabama, without the support of her biological family, and navigate a sometimes-hostile, male-dominated playing field?

To begin the work of naming the women who had a hand in Willie Mae's development, first I had to understand where she belonged as a performer in the context of a multigenerational movement that transcended the classic era and stretched past the blues as a genre. In *Blues People*, Amiri Baraka lays out some of the social and cultural conditions under which the classic blues were formed and how women were professionalized in "the Negro theater: the Black minstrel shows, vaudeville shows, carnivals, and tiny circuses. . . . Minstrelsy and vaudeville not only provided employment for a great many women blues singers, but helped to develop the concept of the professional Negro female entertainer."

There were other ways that women professionalized social commentary using the blues. Davis, in her lyrical analysis of Bessie Smith's "Washwoman's Blues," explains how Black women used the blues to formalize complaints about their employment conditions. "Washwoman's Blues," Davis says, "is a powerfully moving tribute to the countless numbers of African-American women whose toiling hands released their more prosperous white sisters from the drudgery of domestic work. . . . Bessie Smith's rendition of 'Washwoman's Blues' simultaneously memorializes these millions of women and issues a cry of condemnation against the conditions under which they have worked, as well as against the society that restricts them to this type of work." Billie Holiday, Mahalia Jackson, and Tina Turner (among many other Black women musicians) were employed as domestic workers in households managed by white women. The fact that Willie Mae, after her mother's death, secured domestic work in the homes of extended family members and sometimes in the homes of family friends adds one more voice to the chorus of "Washwoman's Blues." Bessie Smith modeled one aspect of the dirty blues, and Willie Mae followed her cues.

A little more than a decade after she began to form words, Willie Mae moved through vaudeville and blues circles, picking up tips, skills, showbiz stories, and valuable lessons. She recalled Bessie Smith and Big Maceo being the first blues singers she heard. During her Sammy Green's Hot Harlem Revue years, when she traveled (in her words to Strachwitz) "all over the South," Willie Mae was billed as the "New Bessie Smith," a title she benefited from though it clashed with her desire to sound unique. She was clear about how seriously she took her vocal signature: "My singing comes from experience, my own experience, my own feeling. I got my own feelings for everything," she told Strachwitz. The desire and ability to sound unique do not negate the influence of Smith and first-wave blueswomen born in the late 1800s like Clara Smith, Sara Martin, Alberta Hunter, Ma Rainey, and Lucille Bogan.

The classic blues influence on Willie Mae is apparent

when you look at the songs that appear multiple times in her catalog and live performances. One example is Lucille Bogan's "Black Angel Blues" (1930). Side B of "Black Angel Blues" is the song "Tricks Ain't Walking No More," which places her in the dirty blues musical class of women who were explicit in singing about the peril (and pleasure) attached to sex work. Bogan's "Black Angel Blues" featured just her voice and a lone piano. The song's title shifted as it was covered over the years. B. B. King popularized the song in 1956 but changed the title to "Sweet Little Angel" because he believed the words "Black Angel" being sung at the height of the civil rights movement were too provocative and possibly offensive. Willie Mae's decision to record Bogan's song on her first studio album, *Big Mama Thornton in Europe* (1965), was a symbolic gesture toward her early training by the first wave of blueswomen. Willie Mae used King's title but sang with Bogan's conviction. On the same album, Willie Mae covered the blues standard "Little Red Rooster," written by Willie Dixon and Howlin' Wolf (Charles Burnett) but inspired by its musical antecedent "If You See My Red Rooster," performed by Charlie Patton and Memphis Minnie (Lizzie Douglas) in 1936. Willie Mae often referred to Memphis Minnie as one of her favorite singers and guitarists. Her "Little Red Rooster" performance most resembles Minnie's version in its phrasing and attitude.

Willie Mae found her voice through exposure to the women who shaped Black popular music. She undoubtedly owned the songs she covered, though ownership is contested in the blues and colored by dual meaning. Davis explains: "Blues songs were never considered the personal property of their composers or the performers.

They were the collective property of the black community, disseminated, like folktales, in accordance with the community's oral tradition. A blues sung by one person and heard, remembered, revised, and resung by another, belonged as much to the second performer as to the first." People like Aretha Franklin, who *owned* Otis Redding's "Respect," and Willie Mae, who owned Jerry Leiber and Mike Stoller's "Hound Dog," understood ownership to mean "distinction" and how it complicates the notion of an original song. As a performer, Willie Mae kept her ear to the streets, searching for songs that moved her and that she believed would move the crowd, which, inevitably, meant covers of previous hits.

The second wave of blueswomen, born in the early 1900s, were critical to Willie Mae's entry into the industry. Blueswomen like Victoria Spivey, Ida Goodson, Bertha Chippie, and Katherine Henderson saw Willie Mae perform as she traveled with Sammy Green's Hot Harlem Revue between the ages of fourteen and twenty-two. Many women identified local talent and trained younger women to become part of the performance family. This, too, is mothering. The earliest labels like Okeh and Columbia used Black people as the first A&R reps to find talent. However, before the labels "discovered" Black vaudeville talent, Black folks were already recruiting one another, as the troupes and revues presented a legitimate way to earn income and escape degrading forms of physical labor (domestic or fieldwork).

Diamond Teeth Mary worked as an A&R rep for Sammy Green's Hot Harlem Revue. Also known as Walking Mary, she was a seasoned performer. By the time she "discovered" Willie Mae singing on that infamous garbage truck, she had already worked for several traveling shows, including Irwin C. Miller's Brown Skin Models, the Davis Bell Medicine Show, and the famous Rabbit Foot Minstrels. Mary worked the tent show for eleven years and shared the stage with other Rabbit Foot veterans such as Ida Cox, Bessie Smith, Louis Jordan, and Ma Rainey. An acrobat and singer from West Virginia, Walking Mary ushered in the next generation of blueswomen, a responsibility that, again, returns us to the concepts of chosen families and mothering. Spörke noted that when Diamond Mary walked into a club to surprise Willie Mae during one of her last performances in the 1980s, Willie Mae shouted from the stage, "With Honor and gentlemen, that's Diamond Mary, she's my mother, she pulled me off of the back of a garbage truck in Alabama."

As a Sammy Green's Hot Harlem Revue member, Willie Mae Thornton was officially part of a Black underground cash economy led by professionally fabulous and streetwise women. The brilliance of these women was connected to the communities who shaped them and who were shaped by them. Costume designers, cooks, hairstylists, tailors, whorehouse mothers, madams, jook joint managers, moonshine and corn liquor operators, promoters, dancers, and entrepreneurs. These blueswomen, the ones Davis describes as embodying "quotidian expressions of feminist consciousness," touched the life of Willie Mae Thornton.

Knowing that these women were part of Willie Mae's formative years takes me back to the question of who she was as a young mother. I want to know the role these women played in the birth of Willie Mae's child. Were any of them midwives? Did they help her through the pregnancy? These are questions of care whose answers escaped the public record. Questions that form an intentional recognition of Willie Mae's humanity and an acknowledgment of perhaps one of the most traumatizing events in her life — the removal of her child by the state. I return to it to honor this moment, not to sensationalize or exploit it. She traveled with, learned from, and listened to comics, chorus girls in line, musicians, and the sex workers that Sammy employed on Atlanta's Decatur Street, and they, regardless of whether they took up the role officially or unconsciously, were responsible for Willie Mae's safety in an adult world. It's also clear that Sammy Green's success would not have been possible without these women and Willie Mae.

Sammy Green was a light-skinned man who, because of his proximity to whiteness, had more access to money and resources than the average dark-skinned Negro in the 1940s. He owned a few rooming houses on Decatur Street. Before forming his revue, Sammy sold popcorn and candy; in time, he moved to selling rooms by the hour for women and their clients. A true hustler, he saved money from side gigs and built the Sammy Green's Hot Harlem Revue, which comprised about fifty people who performed mainly at theaters. The 81 Bailey Theater, also on Decatur, was a prominent Black performance venue that sparked the careers of quite a few famous people. Up until the 1940s, Atlanta, a Black mecca for economic independence, was where many Black stars launched their careers, including Bessie Smith. It was in Atlanta where Willie Mae, Billy Wright, and Little Richard encountered one another.

Even in a city with an established Black entertainment industry, *the money was funny*, as my Big Momma would say—inconsistent at times for reasons outside the performer's control and contingent on the honesty of promoters and showrunners. In Atlanta, Willie Mae became aware that she would have to draw on all her skills to make ends meet, so she started a shoeshine business and found patrons outside local nightclubs. The ingenuity she learned hustling as a child in Alabama and as a teenager in Atlanta carried her from city to city for the next forty years.

That same ingenuity is how Diamond Teeth Mary earned her second title, Walking Mary. In the 1983 documentary *Free Show Tonite*, which features the last living medicine show performers, Mary shares the origin story of her second name: "When I didn't like something, I'd just walk off." She elaborated and discussed walking out on shows produced by unscrupulous promoters. Walking Mary taught Willie Mae the importance of standing your ground when the dirty blues business threatened your dignity and cheated you out of well-earned pay.

In 1948, during a show in Houston, Willie Mae walked out on Sammy Green like Mary would have. "I quit the show in '48," she told Strachwitz. "They owed me a little, well, quite a bit of money, and they wouldn't pay it, and I just got tired." So, Willie Mae hopped off Sammy Green's tour bus and touched down in the middle of another burgeoning music scene in Texas and landed into the care of a new community of blueswomen—and another shady businessman.

Tyina Steptoe explains the appeal of Houston to Black emigrants looking for steady work and chocolate city amenities: "Since World War I, black migrants from Louisiana and East Texas had flocked to Houston to find jobs, as the city began to grow into an economic center because of the export of cotton and oil. By the 1930s, black communities in the city's Third Ward, Fourth Ward, and Fifth Ward had their own entertainment districts." The Black entertainment bubble extended well into the 1970s.

Contrary to the common narrative of Willie Mae's life around her landing in Texas, her story does not begin with Don Robey. It started with Anna Johnson Dupree, one of Willie Mae's sisters of the dirty blues. The Eldorado Ballroom, Dupree's flagship investment, was one of the first and most important Black performance venues in Texas. In Willie Mae's biography, B. B. King explained the significance of the Eldorado to Black artists: "The Eldorado Ballroom, of course, was a big club, with a big dance floor and when you got a chance to play in the Eldorado Ballroom, you hit the big time." Dupree was a Black domestic worker turned businesswoman and philanthropist. Like Mahalia Jackson and Madam C. J. Walker, she made her money as a hairdresser primarily for white Houstonians. She also owned a Turkish bath, a sweatbox, and a massage parlor, among other businesses in the Third Ward. Economic power moves like these exacted revenge for the exploitation chronicled in Bessie Smith's "Washwoman's Blues." They also provided the platform Willie Mae needed to cultivate her talent and reach local listeners. The Eldorado Ballroom hosted James Brown, Ray Charles, Ruth Brown, and other contemporaries who understood the cultural capital that came with being associated with such a well-known venue. Between 1948 and 1950, Willie Mae sang for the saxophonist and bandleader I. H. "Ike" Smalley, who had been a resident musician at the Eldorado Ballroom for nearly ten years. After he left, Willie Mae sang with the next Eldorado house band, the House Rockers, led by

Pluma Davis. Willie Mae's regular performances at the venue solidified her status as Texas music royalty before she signed with a label, just as her work at the 81 Theater bolstered her reputation in Atlanta. Notably, the Eldorado is a key birthplace of what Baraka refers to as working-class R&B, and Willie Mae is a primary reference in its emergence. Performing at the Eldorado and having the support of Anna Johnson Dupree also gave Willie Mae the chance to meet the artists who inspired her and whose songs she frequently covered—Louis Jordan, Fats Domino, and Joe Brown. It was at the Eldorado Ballroom where Willie Mae first encountered Peacock label owner Don Robey.

Robey was the grandson of a plantation owner and an enslaved woman from South Carolina. Early in his life, he worked odd jobs, ranging from cotton farms to docks, before entering the music industry as a club owner in Los Angeles in the 1930s. Like Sammy Green, Robey from an early age proved a skilled hustler with a sharp business acumen who could pass for white. He owned several businesses around Houston, including a taxi service, an amusement parlor, and Sweet Dreams Café. In 1945, with money earned from gambling and side businesses, he opened the Bronze Peacock Dinner Club, another upscale performance hall that catered to the Fifth Ward's middle-class Black community. Robey hired professional chefs and implemented a dress code to emphasize bourgeois aesthetics in his establishment. He also brought in Evelyn Johnson as office manager, though she acted more as a business partner for the Bronze Peacock. In that capacity she became another sister of the dirty blues for young Willie Mae.

Johnson, a blues business–savvy woman, was part of a

family that migrated from Louisiana to the Fifth Ward, an area known for its Creole communities. She cofounded the Peacock dynasty and used her skills as a manager to grow the business and broker deals. In 1949, Johnson developed a new business plan that helped to legitimize Peacock as an independent record label. When Robey struggled to find booking agencies for one of the label's first artists, Clarence "Gatemouth" Brown, Johnson herself applied for a booking license from the American Federation of Musicians. She then established the Buffalo Booking Agency in 1951. The permit allowed Brown and other artists to be booked in Texas and other southern states like Mississippi, Louisiana, and even as far west as Cali.

Evelyn Johnson knew Black artists struggled to attract large audiences, so she partnered with smaller venues to establish a more expansive route for Peacock artists to tour and perform. Johnson was an architect of the Chitlin' Circuit infrastructure. She also worked, though informally, as an A&R rep for Robey. She was partly responsible for signing Clarence "Gatemouth" Brown, the Dixie Hummingbirds, Johnny Ace, the Five Blind Boys, among other artists. On Johnson's watch, Peacock also signed Little Richard, Billy Wright, Marie Adams, and even Betty Carter as part of its jazz division. Later, she oversaw the merging of regional sounds when Robey acquired the Memphis-based Duke Records and inherited several blues and gospel musicians from the Mississippi Delta region. Though it is Don Robey's name that is most associated with this era of Houston music and Willie Mae's first attempt at commercial success, it can rightfully be said that Evelyn Johnson was the queen mother of Texas R&B. To his credit, though, Robey knew to court Willie Mae as soon as possible. Upon hearing about Willie Mae's regular gigs at the Eldorado Ballroom, Robey showed up one evening to watch her perform and immediately invited her to join the Peacock Records family.

Unimpressed and aware of circulating rumors about his shady business practices — such as insisting on writing credit for songs composed by his artists and using violence as a negotiation technique — Willie Mae, in her interview with Strachwitz, said she hesitated before signing with the label. This hesitance speaks to the politics Willie Mae inherited from Diamond Mary. She was ready to walk before she sealed the deal. Her vulnerable position as a blues migrant worker surely incentivized her to sign. Once she did, in 1951, she found herself in a challenging position — just as she had feared.

The management at Peacock wanted to change Thornton's appearance. The singer's penchant for overalls and suits troubled Evelyn Johnson in particular. As the Buffalo Booking Agency manager, Johnson tried to reconstruct Thornton's style into one that fit notions of acceptable Black femininity in the 1950s. According to Steptoe, Johnson wanted Willie Mae to be "like the women featured in African American magazines like *Jet*, which published covers that spotlighted young, thin, light-skinned black women clad in gowns and expensive jewelry." In this way, Johnson's role was less benevolent in that she pushed Willie Mae to conform to a more marketable brand of femininity as shaped by powerful men and patriarchal women.

Willie Mae respected Johnson for recognizing her talent, but she struggled with Johnson's push for acceptable femininity. Discussions about what Willie Mae would wear for any given performance were charged. In Texas,

Willie Mae had become known for her heavy drinking and her so-called aggressive or masculine behavior. She would curse you out; she had the kind of temper that got her in trouble *and* kept her safe; she wore overalls and khaki pants and was unwilling to appease audiences, managers, and associates who wanted to see her be more "ladylike." She had been resisting the trap of ladyhood since 1940 and in Texas, that resistance continued.

In his biography, Spörke shares that Evelyn referred to Willie Mae as a "female thug" and said, "She was very blunt . . . prone to say, 'I ain't wearing that.'" Johnson tried other measures when Willie Mae wouldn't put on a dress. They went to some of the same department stores where Johnson shopped, like Weiner's and Battlestein's, but Willie Mae resisted. "Look here, boss lady, I ain't goin' in there," she'd say. They went to other stores like Foley's and Sakowitz to find bigger clothes and eventually settled on a lace dress. Peacock even hired a woman to dress her, but this arrangement did not work out for Willie Mae or the label.

I see and share this story with Willie Mae — shopping with my mother and protecting my style, resisting suggestions while trying to avoid the charge of ingratitude. I wanted to get school clothes from the boy sections because they made more sense for my breakdance lifestyle. The question is, did traveling with a label chaperone have an impact on Willie Mae's performances? To resist the watchful eye of the label, Willie Mae would sometimes shed the outfits assigned and wear some element of her own clothes by the time she made it to the stage. I, too, would wear to school the clothes my mother picked out for me, then change in the bathroom and return to the playground with my own style. I continued to dress like a Cali B-boy with knee pads and windbreaker jackets, and Willie Mae continued to dress like a Texas bluesman with big-brimmed hats and cowboy boots.

Judging by her persistence, Willie Mae was unphased by speculation about her sexuality. Whatever she wore, she successfully toured the Chitlin' Circuit, causing a riotous stir wherever she landed. She developed a new skill set as a performer, honing her voice between live shows and recording studios. As an artist recording and performing for a label, Willie Mae shifted from being a dynamic entertainer with multiple roles on the vaudeville stage (comedian, dancer, singer, musician) to a lone woman behind the mic. This reduction of Willie Mae's multifaceted stage act worked better for the limited American imagination regarding Black women musicians in the 1950s. The public preferred singers, not musicians or multitalented entertainers.

WHITE BOY MAGIC AND THE MAKING OF GENRE

> Big Mama Thornton didn't follow regular blues forms, sort of like Lightnin' Hopkins. She made her changes when she felt like it. And you just better go along with her. If you weren't fast enough to keep up with her, then too bad.
>
> JOHN KILGORE, RECORDING ENGINEER

> Own boss, own your masters, slaves
>
> JAY-Z, "NO HOOK"

Stevie Wonder introduced me to the harmonica as a Black soul vehicle. And not until I started listening closely to Willie Mae's life did I make the connection between the blues and Stevie's mastery of the mouth organ. My first encounter with Stevie's harmonica was two songs I heard in the 1980s, "Do I Do" from his *Original Musiquarium I* in 1982 and "I Was Made to Love Her," which he cowrote with his mother in 1967 when he was only seventeen. In 1962, at age twelve, "Little Stevie" released a single on Berry Gordy's Tamla Records titled "I Call It Pretty Music, but the Old People Call It the Blues," written by Clarence Paul and Henry Cosby.

There are two parts of the song on each side of the 7-inch version of the record. Part 1 is an up-tempo Motown signature song. It combines pop and R&B elements, creating the "Sound of Young America" that Berry Gordy set out to produce on his assembly line–inspired record company. Part 2 is mainly instrumental, except for Stevie singing the chorus. This version is a slower, more traditional blues, even though it centers the voice and is guided by a child and his harmonica. The song is about how the blues are passed down, directly or indirectly, to new generations. The lyrics don't necessarily separate Stevie from the "old people" in question. It's the teachers who hear him "pla-yin' *in a mellow way*" that identify the music as the blues. His understanding of it as "pretty music" is an exciting way to think about music migration and what happens when the blues travels with migrants to places like Michigan and becomes part of the regional sound through a city's music label. It also points to the fact that regardless of the prominence of blues in Black people's collective listening practices, there has never been a decline in understanding it as a permanent cultural reference or the cornerstone of sonic Blackness. Younger people might call it something else — pretty music — but what can be heard across space and time is a new shaping of the old people's blues.

Stevie Wonder taught himself to play the harmonica at age four in Saginaw, Michigan. He is known for playing a chromatic rather than the more common diatonic harmonica. The chromatic harmonica has up to sixteen holes compared to the ten holes on the diatonic and is much more difficult to master. Factor in his age when he first picked up the harmonica, and it's clear why Little Stevie recorded a live album at the Chicago Regent Theatre in 1963 titled *The 12 Year Old Genius*.

At eight years old, Willie Mae Thornton taught herself to play the harmonica in Alabama. In several interviews, she wore as a badge of honor the fact that she was self-taught and shared with Strachwitz that she "never had no one to teach me nothing. I never went to school for music or nothing. I stayed home to take care of my mother, who was sick. I taught myself to sing and to blow harmonica and even to play the drums by watching other people." She watched her older brother C. W. "Harp" Thornton and landed an old harmonica he had chucked in the trash. Willie Mae mothered herself as a musician. According to her biographer, her brother did not teach or encourage her to play. Her gendered duties were limited to the caretaking of her mom, but that didn't stop her from learning and excelling as a player on her terms. The same set of gender limitations would determine how little harmonica she played in front of live audiences at the beginning of her career. The blues are synonymous with Black men and their guitars; blueswomen are hardly ever associated with an instrument. The decision not to have Willie Mae play harmonica on any of her early Peacock recordings illuminates this point.

Like so many other blues and soul innovators, Willie Mae played the diatonic harmonica and introduced new colors to its voice. Listening to her solos, specifically those at the American Folk Blues Festival in 1965 and her 1971 live performance in Eugene, Oregon, you learn that she makes the harmonica sing as much as it speaks. Despite being discouraged from blowing in favor of singing during her teenage years as a member of a revue and as a young adult on the Chitlin' Circuit in the 1950s, she became an accomplished harmonica blues player nonetheless. I surveyed a slew of top-ten lists on blues harmonica players from reputable music magazines like the *Blues Rock Review*, and not only is Willie Mae missing from many of them but so, too, are any other women. I have yet to find the names of other Black women harmonica players written into blues history, though I know for sure they exist, somewhere on the margins. This uncelebrated aspect of Willie Mae's legacy demands attention. Even though the harmonica is associated most frequently with the blues, it must be said that Willie Mae and Stevie Wonder are fluent in multiple genres and, as such, solidly rooted in their roles as Black music makers. But what do we mean by genre? And how likely is it for Black artists to have the power to name and categorize the sounds they create?

As a college student, I preferred Led Zeppelin and Pink Floyd over H-Town and R. Kelly. I wasn't trying to be the Denise Huxtable alternative girl who looked down on Black youth culture; it was just that these British classic rock bands sounded deeply soulful to me. I didn't listen to them because they were white; I listened because I heard something Black. Maureen Mahon shares a similar experience and talks about the impetus for her study in *Black Diamond Queens: African American Women and Rock and Roll*. "Over the course of researching this book," she writes, "I was surprised to learn how prominently British artists figured in the stories of the African American women I was tracing. The Stones, the Beatles, David Bowie, and Humble Pie have a stronger presence in the text than their American counterparts, and I realized that my personal preference for British rock likely led me to focus on these connections — connections that grew out of British musicians' well-documented fascination with African-American music." Like me, Mahon listened to groups like the Police,

Queen, and the Clash and responded to that sonic pull that spoke to how Black American music crossed the Atlantic to play a foundational role in the British rock that then invaded America.

In the case of the Police, the Clash, and the English Beat, I was confronted by the erasure of Black reggae musicians who were either born in or had migrated to the UK between the 1940s and the 1970s. It's true that some of my first experiences with reggae came from the Caribbean-inflected sound that white UK acts premiered on the American charts. It wasn't until long after I developed a relationship with the Police and the Clash that I discovered groups like Steel Pulse and Aswad and Caribbean artists like Grace Jones and Eddy Grant. Although their one-drop, dub, and ska sounds found a home on American radio through the white bands they influenced, Black British people of African and Caribbean descent were hardly recognized as the originators of the music that was dominating American pop. Learning years later that many of the UK classic rock bands I adored were students of the blues was equally surprising. They borrowed guitar licks, reproduced song structures, and mimicked the styles they heard played by Black country women folk and electric bluesmen.

As Mahon maps out in her book, these artists were drawing on the phrasing, vocal performances, and even dance movements of Black women (see Tina Turner) who laid the foundation for the intonations, arrangements, and Black femme swag that circled American and British rock 'n' roll. Mahon is careful not to limit the discussion of Black women's influence to what she brilliantly names their "vocal labor." She also discusses "creative labor" that

Black women have offered rock in the form of consulting, advising, styling, and directing the professional and sometimes romantic relationships they had with white Brit rockers as well. Pianists like Aretha Franklin and Roberta Flack, guitarists like Rosetta Tharpe and Memphis Minnie, and harpists like Alice Coltrane and Dorothy Ashby influenced British music as well. There was never a time in history when Black women were not shaping white American and white British popular music.

Willie Mae Thornton was among the artists studied by white Americans and Brits for her skills as a singer and multi-instrumentalist. She was also among the first women to travel to Europe with the blues. An investigation into the making of genre sheds light on the fact that while Black women cocreated the music, white gatekeepers created genre to control it. Hundreds of Black women performers were pushed into obscurity when their blues-rock-funk wasn't enough — white or Black or male enough — to convince the gatekeepers of the rock establishment of their "worthiness."

The question I've found myself returning to when it comes to Willie Mae is, what genre can contain the music created by a poor Black southern gender-nonconforming woman shaped by vaudeville revues, gospel quartets, the Chitlin' Circuit, Mississippi Delta and Chicago blues, and Texas R&B? I've contemplated the political nature of genre, the unique space that Willie Mae occupied, as well as the price she, like many of her contemporaries (LaVern Baker, Ruth Brown, etc.), paid for existing betwixt and between genre and for living comfortably outside the boxes created for them, not by them. Most importantly, however, I'm interested in how white men — like magic — have maintained dominance over how Black artists are named, marketed, sold, produced, recorded, critiqued, and reviewed. I'm also interested in how they've been able to own Black music masters — both people and albums, to which Jay-Z's "No Hook" refers. By "magic," I mean the white-supremacist, capitalist patriarchy, as bell hooks called it for decades before her passing. The magic is in the shape-shifting invincibility of that system and how it hides behind the curtain of racial progress.

There's a line that stands out to me from the 1995 film *Friday*, which has remained a legitimate reference point for many Black Angelenos for two decades now. It's the part when Big Worm rolls up on Smokey and Craig while they're chillin' on the porch. He's expecting payment for a weed deal made where he fronted Smokey the product, assuming the money would be returned on the back end. This is the life of underground cash economies — one based on honor systems and principles, or as Big Worm would say, "the principalities." With his perfectly parted hair and the five rows of aqua blue one-inch rollers covering the circumference of his head, Big Worm looks Smokey in the eye and says, "Playing with my money is like playing with my emotions." The labor of collecting payment angers him. The writers of this film, DJ Pooh and Ice Cube (before he met with Trump), understood the resonance of a Big Worm character in working-class Black neighborhoods like Compton and Crenshaw. The areas where I, Ice Cube, and DJ Pooh resided in the '80s and the '90s. Linking money to emotion is a particular way of thinking about what happens to the heart when people have, throughout your career, played games with your money. Through Willie Mae's life, I have learned that this is what drives the emotional underworld of capitalism: the need for capital to do what you love, and the way that being underpaid can turn you against what you love. There's money, of course, and then there's the *social* capital granted by industry insiders and peripheral players like journalists, television hosts, and DJs.

Willie Mae's prospects of commercial success were contingent on a series of white men. Two popular ones stand out. The first was a Brooklynite working for *Billboard* magazine named Jerry Wexler. He was credited with coining the term "rhythm and blues" just one year after Willie Mae left Sammy Green's Hot Harlem Revue and signed with Peacock. Though Wexler was responsible for launching the careers of artists such as Wilson Pickett and Led Zeppelin, I became familiar with him through his role as a producer of note after he set the stage for the golden (Atlantic) years of Aretha Franklin (1966–72). Wexler signed on as a partner for Atlantic Records in 1953. As a producer, he tapped into the talent that Columbia Records, Aretha's previous label, couldn't actualize (though many fans appreciate those early Aretha recordings of blues and jazz standards). No one can deny that Wexler understood how a focus on funk and soul music would enhance her already highly developed skills as a pianist and vocalist. But what Wexler did that calls for closer examination was deny Aretha's request to receive a production credit for her creative genius in the studio. This was indeed playing with her music, her money, and, yes, her emotions. Eventually, after producing much of her music for Atlantic since 1967 (with support from her sister Carolyn Franklin and a team of studio musicians), she fought for and finally received coproduction credit for the *Amazing Grace* album in 1972.

Aretha took control of that Black church project. Under her *formal* production leadership, *Amazing Grace* became her highest-selling album to date.

Ten years before Wexler worked with Aretha, Alan Freed, a DJ and concert promoter, was an active proponent of naming Black people as architects of rock 'n' roll. Alan Freed popularized the term "rock 'n' roll" in 1951, though it appeared in *Billboard* magazine as early as 1946 to describe new music by the Black group Joe Liggins and His Honey-drippers. As the story goes, the term did not catch on until Alan Freed used it. This also speaks to the magic of how words, genres, peoples, countries, and continents don't exist until white men "discover" them. What Freed did that was radical, for his time, was play R&B tunes under the rock 'n' roll banner. His intentions in doing this can be found on his website as an official statement for his foundation: "Rock and roll is really swing with a modern name. It began on the levees and plantations, took in folk songs, and features blues and rhythm."

Freed used his radio program, the *Moondog Show* on WJW in Cleveland, to play the original (Black) versions of songs that white cover musicians were popularizing. Often, the songs he featured were released by small, independent record labels, very much like Peacock Records, which recorded Willie Mae. Freed addressed the politics of cultural extraction that set the stage for folks like Elvis Presley, the Pat Boone Family, and Jerry Lee Lewis. White-faced Black sound was a profitable preference, institutionalized through a concerted effort between major record labels, music magazines, television outlets, and radio stations.

Alan Freed's decision to play Black artists on his radio show and to produce televised revues gave exposure to artists such as Ruth McFadden, Frankie Lymon, Big May-belle, the Platters, and Chuck Berry, now recognized as "early influences" of multiple genres of popular American music. He used some of his magic for good and helped Americans hear what they needed to hear: that rock 'n' roll is rhythm & blues, meaning it is Black music. Jerry Wexler and Alan Freed deserve credit for using their resources — exclusively available to white men — to introduce the world to some of the most important names in Black music. With those same resources, they were afforded the power to name the music created by Black people, to determine where that music should be placed on industry publication charts (like *Billboard* and radio), and to decide who would be credited the music's producer. Both Jerry Wexler and Alan Freed were inducted into the Rock and Roll Hall of Fame. While it's essential to understand their role in the popularization of mid-twentieth-century Black music, the accolades and wealth still eclipse that of the music's Black creators. And that of Willie Mae.

The differences between Wexler and Freed don't matter to history. At the end of the day, ever-resourced white men within the music industry continue to have endless access. However, I recognize that they were on opposite ends of the battlefield: Wexler represented the interests of big record companies and music publishers, while Freed represented one of the biggest threats to those institutions, the honest crediting and platforming of those responsible for shaping what was being called rock 'n' roll. Freed died with mounting reputational damage from his involvement with payola schemes and related tax-evasion charges. Wexler became one of the most celebrated men in record-ing industry history. This is how genres are born and how people are disappeared from their cultural products when white boy magic is centered. Unfortunately, many artists they helped introduce, produce, record, and support died poor and unremembered. And many of them, including Willie Mae, were never inducted to the Rock and Roll Hall of Fame.

In addition to fighting against respectability politics and dress codes while in Texas, Willie Mae earned a reputation for responding violently to the unsavory business practices of promoters and, eventually, Black-owned record labels, which modeled their businesses after shady white record company men. In the Charles White biography *The Life and Times of Little Richard*, Little Richard spoke to Willie Mae's force in business matters: "Robey was known for beating people up. He would beat everybody up but Big Mama Thornton. He was scared of her, and she was built like a big bull." As disappointing as his choice of words is in referencing her size, he points to a woman who could protect herself from dangerous situations. I'm not sure she fully escaped the underworld elements of the 1950s independent label industry, but Little Richard's observations offer me solace. Unfortunately, Little Richard was not immune to Robey's dangerous management style. In the same biography, he described being brutally beaten by the unscrupulous executive. Eventually, Little Richard signed with Specialty Records, which bought out his contract from Peacock. Robey could be a bully with his business and his body. Several artists wrote about or shared oral histories on their experiences with Robey. Johnny Otis, a famous bandleader and musician who became a lifelong friend to Willie Mae, was one of them.

When Johnny Otis stopped in Houston to perform with

his traveling Rhythm and Blues Caravan from Los Angeles, Robey reached out with a proposition. He requested that Otis audition his Peacock artists hoping that Otis would help to launch their careers. Otis agreed, and Willie Mae Thornton and her labelmate Marie Adams left Houston to tour with Otis in 1952. As part of the deal, Otis was to oversee Peacock-sponsored recording sessions scheduled to take place in Los Angeles. The most important aspect of the agreement, which adds layers to the lore surrounding the song "Hound Dog," was that Robey insisted that Otis hand over all the finished masters—the source material (original recording) from which copies of a song, album, or performance are made. Otis agreed.

I'm not sure where to place Johnny Otis as it relates to race, but I know that his role in the "Hound Dog" story gets lost in translation. So does his legacy, enduring friendship with, and respect for Willie Mae as well as his commitment to the quality of life for the Black musicians he worked with and learned from in the Los Angeles area. Otis and his fellow musicians entertained themselves between shows by playing baseball and competing with local athletes starting in the late 1940s. Willie Mae Thornton was especially moved by the softball games and the community of people she could, once again, make a home with and rely on, even if that support was just recreational.

There's a lot of talk about cultural appropriation in the history of the music industry. Many of those discussions are flattened by a limited analysis of how white privilege and the history of Black people's social position as property come into play when discussing the notion of stealing culture. What does it mean to steal from someone who lives in a country that refuses to address the legacies of slavery? Or the fact that the very people whose culture is being stolen or appropriated were stolen themselves? I'm interested in how this plays out in the life of Johnny Otis.

Born Ioannis Alexandres Veliotes in Vallejo, California, to Greek immigrants, Johnny Otis was the first Black-passing figure that crossed into my world. Before learning more about Otis, I assumed he was Black. Even upon seeing him in photos with Willie Mae taken during their softball games. Given the racial ambiguity I observed, I was keen to learn about how Johnny Otis navigated Willie Mae's artistic might and her vulnerabilities. According to Otis's biographer, George Lipsitz, "Otis considered Big Mama Thornton one of the best people and one of the most impressive musicians he ever encountered. He saw her cheated out of royalties by unscrupulous record company executives, exploited by nightclub owners, and unacknowledged by artists who copied features of her act." Lipsitz placed Otis in a different category from the white men (Wexler and Freed) who had a say in Willie Mae's success, even if indirectly by setting the terms for where popular Black music could be assessed for its marketability and heard by the general public. "Like Johnny Otis," Lipsitz says, "many of the white people engaged in producing, promoting, and selling rhythm and blues music after World War II had been members of immigrant ethnic households in the 1930s. . . . Many of these men made a fortune from Black music, but among them, only Johnny Otis became an actual part of the Black community and its political, religious, and cultural life."

Otis knew he was white but thought of himself as "Black by persuasion," he confessed in Lipsitz's biography. That's how Ioannis Alexandres Veliotes became Johnny Otis.

Unsurprisingly, he married a Black Filipino woman named Phyllis. Their son Shuggie was a prodigy guitarist and multi-instrumentalist hailed as Hendrix's heir. It's possible that Phyllis's memories are fraught with complicated feelings. The question of race remains a complicated one; so, too, does the question of mothering.

Johnny's mother, Irene, refused to speak to her daughter-in-law for fifteen years because she hated that he had married a Black woman. This is one place where Otis's whiteness becomes abundantly clear.

Johnny Otis launched careers, employed new talent, played predominantly Black music on his radio show on KFOX in Southern California, and had his own television show. He rarely accepted solo gigs, preferring to roll with a crew of Black musicians he knew needed exposure. His relationship with the Black church led to him becoming a minister of his congregation, and his activist work on LAPD brutality was well documented in several publications. Still, nothing could have prepared me for learning that he wrote a column for the *Los Angeles Sentinel*. My grandmother from Mississippi sat with the *Sentinel* nightly while drinking Folgers instant coffee or eating a bowl of cornbread and buttermilk. I wonder if she read his articles. I wonder if, because of his political conviction, my grandmother assumed Otis was Black too. Sometimes the words in his column were indeed written by Black Angelenos, as he interviewed local activists and scholars to amplify their perspective and aid their organizing efforts.

Here's what I know. Otis was a human being indoctrinated into the system of white supremacy. I do not believe he could escape what it means to be born into whiteness, and I do not claim to know his blind spots or his complicity in whiteness and the institutionalized racism and history of exploitation that defines the American music industry. But based on extensive research and testimonies by many Black artists, including Willie Mae, I get the sense that he had meaningful, and hopefully honest relationships with the Black artists he worked with. One can only hope. And I say "hope" very intentionally. On the one hand, touring with Otis's Caravan was an amazing opportunity for Willie Mae. She was introduced to a broader audience and stretched herself as an artist. Her Los Angeles recording studio sessions, however, are a cautionary tale. Because of our collective focus on Elvis Presley for decades, Robey has escaped scrutiny for possibly cheating Willie Mae. Otis's role in the infamous recording session still isn't fully clear to me.

I use the word "hope" with Otis because I'm aware that taking production or songwriting credit was standard practice among many label executives, Black ones included. Anita Baker and Nina Simone share a troubling history. They both had husbands who managed them and took publishing credit or royalty money earned by the women themselves. In addition to her challenge with Wexler, Aretha's husband was among the men who received songwriting credit and royalty checks from her labor. So, when I say I "hope" Otis was honest, it is because I cannot ignore that he, too, was accused of benefiting from this system. Etta James, whom Otis is said to have "discovered," accused him of taking credit for the song "Work with Me Annie." In her memoir (ghostwritten by David Ritz) she shares her side of the story: "Johnny claimed co-authorship to make more money from the record." Otis biographer George Lipsitz reports that "Otis insists that he never gave himself songwriting credit unless he participated meaningfully in the creation of a song."

My hope is informed by questions about songwriting credit and publishing that have been hovering around record labels for centuries. The more I've looked into the history of the labels, the more enraged I've become about the exploitive slavery conditions that enshrine the publishing industry. Aside from publishing credit is the question of music business literacy, and discussions of literacy for Black people are bound up with the legacy of slavery, too. Early blues and R&B artists belonged to a community of people who were punished or killed for learning how to read. Let's be clear: the cheating, the payment in alcohol, and the hidden and fine-print fees that artists found themselves responsible for are all extensions of sharecropping capitalism, another invention of white boy magic.

GROWN LITTLE GIRLS, TOMBOY WOMEN, AND BLACK RADIO

It's been thirty years and I've never done the
same show twice. Honestly, I think I'm one of the
worst entertainers. Also, the same clothes I wear
during the day, that might be the same shit I wear
on stage. I don't have a glam squad. I still don't
know how to wear makeup. I never became that
entertainer.

ROXANNE SHANTÉ

I'm part of a community of folk raised in the "golden era"
of hip-hop who pride themselves on paying homage to
anyone with proven freestyle skills. As a young girl growing up in Los Angeles, I was consumed by the legendary
freestyle skills of Roxanne Shanté. A precocious girl from
the New York Queensbridge projects, Roxanne Shanté
had no business throwing the first lyrical punch at the rap
group Untouchable Force Organization (UTFO) with her
debut song "Roxanne's Revenge," produced by DJ Marley Marl. In the spirit of dancehall riddims, "Roxanne's
Revenge" was recorded over the original (though slightly
manipulated) instrumental version of UTFO's "Roxanne

Roxanne," produced by Full Force, which sampled Billy Squier's "Big Beat." The song was about a fictitious woman who refused to engage catcalls from men (presumably UTFO). Legend has it that Roxanne, a teenager at the time, recorded the entire song as a seven-minute freestyle in one take between washing laundry.

Willie Mae could spit lyrics off the dome just as well as Roxanne, and she knew it. Echoing the sentiment of Roxanne Shanté's quote, noting the strength of her strategic unpredictability, Willie Mae shared, "Now, on the stage, I can perform forty minutes and never say the same thing twice," she told Strachwitz. "See, it just comes to me like that. I can just start to singing and make a song right on the stage. And I think just making up a song on the stage and you get that feeling and got somebody behind you that groove you, it comes out much better anyway." Willie Mae was field hollering on the M-I-C with more than twelve bars and couldn't be clocked by the convenient categories of a finicky industry. No two live versions of her songs are the same. She shifted the context of a tune by giving it a new introduction, as she did quite often with "Ball 'n' Chain." On one version she'd say, "This is the true ball 'n' chain." In another version she'd say, "I wrote this song for the late great Janis Joplin." In another version, like the one she performed for the Ann Arbor Blues Festival in 1969, she introduced "Ball 'n' Chain" by saying "This is what they call a surprise song." Instead of mentioning Janis, she directed the band through a psychedelic rendering of the tune. In the middle of the song, she referred to herself in the third person and changed the lyrics to "You know I don't mean no harm honey, but Big Mama, Big Mama, Big Mama, just don't want to go insane." She thrived on stage when given a chance to improvise.

Willie Mae spent eight years on the revue scene, and like most revues of that era, hers was more like a variety show or circus featuring performances centered around humor and spectacle. Willie Mae, like Bessie Smith, was trained as a singer, a dancer, and a comedian—art forms that rely heavily on improvisation; art forms that made her a standout artist for the duration of her career; and art forms that would have made her an outstanding rapper or emcee. Daphne Duval Harrison speaks to this spontaneity and the making of blues aesthetics: "Two qualities highly valued in the black community, articulateness and toughness, are thus brought together in the art form. Fluency in language is considered a powerful tool for establishing and maintaining status in the black community. Thus, a man or woman who has mastered the art of signifying, rapping, and orating can subdue any challenger without striking a blow and is held in high esteem." This was the Willie Mae Thornton who showed up at Johnny Otis's garage rehearsal space in Los Angeles on August 12, 1952.

Willie Mae was introduced to but unimpressed by two seventeen-year-old Jewish boys whom Johnny Otis invited to watch her perform. Following the chatter among LA artists in the Central Avenue jazz and R&B scene, he recruited the young duo to write a song for her. Once she moved past her initial reservations, she was ready to sing and ad lib, just as any great freestyler would be. The teenagers in Otis's garage that day were Jerry Leiber and Mike Stoller. The pair (both born in 1933) had met in Los Angeles as college students in 1950. Brought together by their love for Black music, namely boogie-woogie, blues, and R&B, they soon entered a songwriting partnership and tried their hand at writing for Black artists in particular.

Lyricist Lieber and composer Stoller struck gold in

writing "Hound Dog" for Willie Mae. They rose to fame thanks to the music industry "old boys' network." Atlantic Records executives Ahmet Ertegun and Jerry Wexler were impressed by the repertoire of songs credited to the duo by 1955. They signed a contract with Atlantic and secured the first-ever independent production deal in the industry. Leiber and Stoller have received countless awards and honors for their extraordinary songbook, which includes hugely successful compositions written for the Coasters, Ben E. King, the Drifters, and over twenty songs for Elvis including "Jailhouse Rock."

They, too, are among the cohort of magical white boys who found a way, through both talent and privilege, to generate millions for themselves through their affiliation with and production of Black music. And like Johnny Otis, Jerry Wexler, and Alan Freed, Leiber and Stoller were inducted into several prestigious halls of fame (Songwriters Hall of Fame, 1985; Record Producer Hall of Fame, 1986; Rock and Roll Hall of Fame, 1987). By 1988, Presley's recording of "Hound Dog" was placed in the Grammy Hall of Fame. They've been compensated in every way possible for their involvement with Black music.

In their memoir, Leiber and Stoller recall meeting Willie Mae that day in August. They heard her sing and then rushed home to write what came up for them musically and lyrically. Excited by the power of her voice, they scribbled down lyrics and wrote "Hound Dog" in a matter of minutes. What happened later that day is a story Leiber told in multiple interviews throughout his career. They returned to the rehearsal space, shared the lyrics with Otis and Willie Mae, and attempted to direct her phrasing and approach to the song. She responded unfavorably. "Maybe if you attack it with a little more — " Leiber said. To which, before he finished, Willie Mae responded, "Come here, boy. I'll tell you what you can attack," while motioning toward her crotch area and finishing him off with "You can attack this."

The entire band that was assembled that day (Pete Lewis on guitar, Johnny Otis on drums, and a bass player named Mario Delagarde) laughed at the exchange and understood Willie Mae as more than a monstrously aggressive woman — language that's been assigned to Black women for the past four hundred years. They understood that embedded in her response to Leiber and Stoller was a comical way of protecting her dignity, an iteration of signifyin'. Willie Mae's attitude in the "Hound Dog" rehearsal session that day reflects and reinforces a consensus that many musicians felt in the 1950s, which was that a measure of caution was needed when working with white folk in the industry. She exercised that same caution the next day when they recorded the song. The caution was more like premonition — a mixture of intuition, experience, and intelligence.

In Lieber and Stoller's joint memoir, Stoller shared his first impressions on the day they met Willie Mae: "She was formidable and a bit frightening. Her voice was a force of nature. Big Mama was absolutely magnificent." Leiber echoed his partner's sentiment: "There was something monstrous about Big Mama. But I wasn't looking at her that way." In Spörke's biography on Willie Mae, Lieber shared even more revealing impressions: "We saw Big Mama, and she knocked me cold. She looked like the biggest, badass, saltiest chick you would ever see. And she was mean, a 'lady bear' as they used to call 'em. She must have been 350 pounds, and she had all these scars all over her face. I had to write a song for her that basically said, 'Go fuck yourself' but how do you do it without actually saying it?" Stoller went on to describe how "Hound Dog" was written with Willie Mae's appearance in mind: "She was a wonderful blues singer with a great moaning style, but it was as much her appearance as her blues style that influenced the writing of 'Hound Dog' and the idea that we wanted her to growl it, which she rejected at first." Willie Mae never concedes to growling; instead, she *hollers* on "Hound Dog." Lieber and Stoller missed this nuanced distinction.

Leiber and Stoller described the tension in the studio on August 13 and how Willie Mae, upon first reading the lyrics the day before, had a different approach in mind. She read the song as a ballad as opposed to the "deadly blues" they intended. When they entered the studio to record, Willie Mae, like any great emcee or revue-trained blueswoman, began improvising: "So I started to sing the words, and I put in some of my own. All that talkin' and hollerin', that's my own," she told Strachwitz. Willie Mae employs a cache of vocal devices to make the song her own. Her ad-libs ("Come here, Daddy!"), the call and response she initiates with the guitarists, and other Black English words she injects leave the songwriters confused, unable to decode, though her additions were just as credible as the lyrics Leiber and Stoller scribbled on a piece of paper in a few minutes.

Willie Mae should have received some publishing credit for the ad-libs. While they were improvised, they were audible words that are part of the song's lyrics. More revealing is that the original lyrics—written by two Jewish boys—included lines about chicken and watermelon. Johnny Otis's decision to scrap those lyrics hid the songwriters' whiteness. In his biography Otis recalled, "Parts of it weren't really acceptable. I didn't like that reference to chicken and watermelon and said, 'Let's get that crap out of there.'" The chicken and watermelon references reveal Leiber and Stoller's limited (and racist) imagination about Blackness, though that limitation didn't prevent them from making their fortune. Still, "Hound Dog" was produced in two takes, a little longer than the time it took to do laundry, if your name is Roxanne Shanté. Yet, "Roxanne's Revenge" holds a unique place in this discussion because she wrote and therefore owned all the song's lyrics.

The question of ownership and signature is complicated. Artists like Aretha Franklin make that clear. Her cover of Otis Redding's "Respect" is the perfect example of how ownership is assumed. The average listener simply knows that regardless of who wrote, sang, or produced it, Aretha *owns* it. And by similar standards, Willie Mae *owns* "Hound Dog." The song became one of the most significant accomplishments and heartbreaks in Willie Mae's career. If she had received a measly 2 percent of the proceeds earned from the song, the quality of her life would have been drastically improved. "Hound Dog" made these men rich while contributing to Willie Mae's skewed life chances.

Leiber and Stoller talked about their love for Willie Mae repeatedly in interviews throughout their career, but they never deemed it necessary to make the legal accommodations to share even a tiny percentage of the profit garnered from "Hound Dog." The references to chicken and watermelon in the original song and the offensive words they used to describe Willie Mae, are aligned with racialized descriptions of Black people in nineteenth-century American literature as detailed in Toni Morrison's critical nonfiction work *Playing in the Dark: Whiteness and the Literary Imagination*. As Morrison points out, language likens Blackness to monsters, creatures, and larger-than-life beings, which are attractive, intriguing, and valuable in their ability to generate resources through labor but somehow less human, less deserving of rightful compensation.

This warped understanding of Blackness from Leiber and Stoller makes its way into their autobiography. Throughout the book, for example, Leiber references Black women as chicks and gals, talks about where he met Black women he dated, how he dated Puerto Ricans. Mahon addresses this racialized bravado in her book when she names the number of white rockers who discuss (either through lyrics or memoirs) their sexual exploits with Black women. These conversations typically happen in tandem with their expressions of love for the music that Black men produce. Leiber and Stoller were in the business of Black life and it paid—both personally and professionally. But it's important to note that their book never once mentions let alone rejects the social conditions that Black people faced, which inevitably informed Black music as a whole.

"Roxanne's Revenge" was officially released as a single by a Philadelphia-based, Black-owned label called Art Pop Records, founded by Lawrence Goodman and his brother Daniel (aka Dana) in 1984. Lawrence Goodman is listed as the producer on the release, and UTFO and Full Force are credited as writers (rightfully so, as they wrote the original that spawned the response). However, Roxanne Shanté and Marley Marl were not credited as producers or songwriters. According to Jesse Serwer of *Wax Poetics*, Goodman, like Don Robey, signed contracts with artists that listed him as full producer even when he was only an executive producer and didn't assemble any beats or write any rhymes.

Though they were worlds, regions, and decades apart, Roxanne Shanté and Willie Mae were cheated out of royalties for records that changed the face of both Black music and popular music in general. In an interview with the *Daily News*, Shanté said, "Everybody was cheating with the contracts, stealing and telling lies. And to find out that I was just a commodity was heartbreaking." Describing yourself as a commodity while belonging to a people once enslaved is no small thing. It recalls Prince donning the word "slave" on his face while in public and refusing to utter his former stage name. His new name, The Artist Formerly Known as Prince, was an act of stealing himself away, like the old Negro spiritual song that mobilized plantation rebellion. His 1995 *Emancipation* album was a declaration of freedom upon being "released" from Warner Music Group.

Willie Mae, who was older than Roxanne when she recorded "Hound Dog," was accustomed to the industry's exploitive nature, which is to say that financial vulnerability, not ignorance of the business per se, informed her career decisions. Many artists signed away their rights to take care of immediate life needs. Some of them had to compromise and leverage financial stability. Willie Mae agreed to Robey's unfair recording contract. What remains undeniable is that what Willie Mae did alone as an artist created the wealth for all the men involved. Willie Mae and Roxanne Shanté's studio work as emcees and writers (even if some of the words were spoken instead of written) made both songs epic and invaluable to the genre and the industry.

At the beginning of her reign, Roxanne Shanté decrowned the proverbial rap kings, setting the foundation for what would become the "Roxanne Wars." At least one hundred answer songs emerged from Shanté's original sonic dagger. Willie Mae's "Hound Dog" sparked a war of its own too. At least six answer songs surfaced following its release, the most famous one written by Rufus Thomas called "Bear Cat," released by Sun Records in 1953. Mahon explains how this hurt Willie Mae: "The competition from the covers and R&B singer Rufus Thomas's answer song 'Bear Cat,' coupled with the limited distribution and airplay available to recordings by black artists in the early 1950s, stalled Thornton's reach on the charts." "Hound Dog" was number 1 on the Black charts for seven weeks. Willie Mae's biographer reported that Robey had three new pressing plants running full blast to keep up with the demand for Willie Mae's record, which sold somewhere between 500,000 and 750,000 copies. Additionally, Robey sued Sun Records over Thomas's answer song. He threatened labels about their imitation responses and warned that "Hound Dog" was the original. Robey won the lawsuit against Sun Records and was awarded 2 percent of all "Bear Cat" profits plus court costs. Although the popularity of "Hound Dog" and the reactions it spawned were directly related to Willie Mae's audacious delivery—her breathing life into the song beyond how it was initially presented—Robey didn't share the 2 percent of "Bear Cat" profits with Willie Mae either.

Johnny Otis believed he was compromised too. Otis claims that he was initially given half the publishing rights and one-third of the songwriting credit because of his role in the studio. Once Presley covered "Hound Dog" in 1956, Leiber and Stoller shifted from their original business agreement with Otis in 1952, arguing that they were minors at the time of the deal. Otis's words on the matter present a chilling picture of the songwriters milking the song for all it was worth: "They sued me in court. They won; they beat me out of it. I could have sent my kids to college like they sent theirs," he says in his biography. Otis did more than remove the offensive lyrics and arrange the drums. He also changed the chorus and removed the horn parts, which created the room to place Willie Mae's voice at the song's center. Leiber and Stoller admitted that they agreed to offer Otis one-third of the mechanical rights on record sales (not on radio or television airplay). However, according to Lipsitz, they still claimed to own all the composition rights. Finally, to secure their wealth following Presley's release of "Hound Dog," they insisted on a new agreement that gave them 46.25 percent of the song while allocating Don Robey 28.75 percent and giving Elvis Presley the remaining 25 percent. The court accepted the decision.

In addition to asserting her "creative labor" in changing the song's intention, phrasing, and vocal arrangements, Willie Mae never backed away from the fact that she believed that Peacock Records and Don Robey failed to pay her the royalties she deserved. In interviews, she repeats the offense throughout her career: "All I made was $500 off of 'Hound Dog,'" she told Strachwitz. Mahon's summary of what the song was able to achieve as a cultural force speaks to how egregious Robey's snub to Willie Mae really was:

["Hound Dog"] was the first major success for Robey's Peacock Records, an example of a lucrative black-owned label several years ahead of Motown's arrival. It was the first hit song for Leiber and Stoller, two of rock 'n' roll's most celebrated songwriters. Backed with "Don't Be Cruel," "Hound Dog" was Presley's biggest-selling single, establishing him as a dominant force in rock 'n' roll and popular music generally. The cross-racial exchange that contributed to Presley's version of "Hound Dog" is an early example of what became a common practice of white male rock 'n' roll artists borrowing from the sound and style of black women.

The million-dollar cover catapulted Presley into a whirlwind of wealth and fame. With that, Robey became to Willie Mae what Marly Marl was to Roxanne; what Berry Gordy was to Mary Wells, Florence Ballard, and Tammi Terrell; what Puffy was to Lil' Kim and Mary J. Blige — men who became wealthy music moguls with the help of talented women.

There is poetry in the parallel experiences of Willie Mae and Roxanne Shanté. Willie Mae Thornton died in 1984, the same year Roxanne Shanté's life as a battle rapper began. It was almost as if a torch were passed on — an Olympic flame of fiery talent based on what Black women witness and testify about on wax. Today, at fifty-three years old, Roxanne Shanté, when she speaks about her influence on the rap game, is just as rebellious as she was at fourteen. Still, in the spirit of artists like Lauryn Hill, Sade, Rihanna, and D'Angelo, Roxanne Shanté, with all her proverbial trophies, left the game (for twenty-five years) while at the height of her success. In a 2018 interview with *VladTV* she explained, "The reason why [I left] was because I had never gotten a royalty check for any of the songs I recorded." When asked how it was possible to be robbed given her success and her part in laying the foundation for hip-hop as a genre, she replied, "It's hard to tell your manager that the record company is doing you dirty when your manager is your record company and when the accountant is the record company's brother."

There is a silver lining connecting these women's stories based on a combination of the facts and my imagination. The thread that binds the two (in my mind) is Shanté's 1992 comeback album, *The Bitch Is Back*, released in 1992, which featured the single "Big Mama." The song doesn't reference Willie Mae, nor is it a tribute to her legacy. But like Walking Diamond (Willie Mae's play mama who pulled her off that garbage truck and was known to walk away from shady business deals), Shanté hints at her own role as the mother of hip-hop, explains why she walked away, and announces her return: "Queen of emceein' / Whenever I flow it's poetry in motion / So you can save all the drama / And get the fuck out the way / Here comes the Big Mama." The chorus is the kicker: "Mama — mama — aww! / I gave birth to most of them MCs." Willie Mae won many battles at package show competitions in the fifties, and she heard how "Hound Dog" covers failed in comparison to her original. And if it's true what Mahon says, that "Hound Dog" helped "establish the sound of rock 'n' roll" and that Willie Mae "is an important foremother of rock 'n' roll," then like Shanté, Willie Mae Thornton was mother to most of them rock 'n' roll MCs.

Black radio is another thread that connects the two. The

first time Willie Mae heard "Hound Dog" was in 1953, a good while after it had been recorded. In the same interview with Chris Strachwitz she shared, "I was going to the theater in Ohio, and I just turned the radio on in the car, and the man said, 'Here's a record that's going nationwide: "Hound Dog" by Willie Mae Thornton.' I said that's me!" Shanté's biopic, *Roxanne Roxanne*, dramatizes the first time she heard "Roxanne's Revenge" played on WBHI's *Rap Attack* radio show with DJ Mr. Magic in 1984. The scene featured the moment when close friends excitedly called her house in the wee hours of the night to alert Shanté that she was on the radio. Thanks to Black radio Willie Mae Thornton and Roxanne Shanté stayed on the Black charts, and because of Black radio DJs, I had a collection of recorded rap shows on cassette that I listened to like albums. Several of those cassettes featured "Roxanne's Revenge" and another Shanté favorite, "Have a Nice Day." I knew and know each song verbatim to this day.

DON'T ASK ME NO MORE ABOUT ELVIS

Couldn't be anything worse than being famous the world over for something you don't even understand.

GRACIE MAE STILL

In the dedication portion of Alice Walker's collection of short stories *You Can't Keep a Good Woman Down*, she honors the blues voodoo queens and songwriters who mothered her vision: "I thank Ma Rainey, Bessie (*A Good Man Is Hard to Find*) Smith, Mamie Smith and Perry (*You Can't Keep a Good Man Down*) Bradford, among others of their generation, for insisting on the value and beauty of the authentic." It's no wonder that "Nineteen Fifty-Five," inspired by the life of Willie Mae Thornton, is the first piece in the collection. Within this short story, Walker's radical imagination creates a protective forcefield around Willie Mae's dignity. "Nineteen Fifty-Five" moves Willie Mae beyond the lifelong and even posthumous victim position and pushes us to unlearn Elvis as the victor.

When the opportunity presented itself to right the wrongs enacted on Willie Mae, I planned to place a literary hit on Elvis and build a case about how his success was shorthand for cultural theft. I was ready to point out the American appetite for hearing and feeling Black people but not seeing them. Which I believe, undoubtedly, is true. Alice Walker, however, does something with the history between Elvis and Willie Mae that blurs the line between revenge fantasy and speculative blues fiction. I trust Alice because of the feeling I had when I met Shug Avery in Walker's 1982 novel *The Color Purple*. More than a character, Shug was a model for the generations of "Wild Women Who Don't Have the Blues" Ida Cox sang about. Hearing Alice Walker describe her vision of Shug Avery in an interview with Charlie Rose taught me that Gracie Mae Still, the protagonist in "Nineteen Fifty-Five," is closer to Walker's Shug Avery than the one portrayed in the 1985 film. Though she appreciated Margaret Avery's portrayal, in Walker's imagination, "Shug was a southern woman who would have been much bigger, she would have had a real full-body." Shug, in her mind, resembled Willie Mae.

"Nineteen Fifty-Five" is a staged intervention that draws on blues history, Willie Mae Thornton's agency, and the network of people and systems who put Elvis on the world stage. Gracie Mae and Traynor as characters are easy to understand as Willie Mae and Elvis. A fictional intimate friendship between the two makes the point that Elvis's status as king was indeed a fatal burden. Walker also uses the story to balance the way Willie Mae Thornton is described as forever bitter about her career. She renders Gracie Mae a figure who has risen above the limitations of a woman scorned. Instead, she is someone who successfully walked away from her blues journey and into the arms of family, love, and stability. The fact that Gracie Mae is partnered with men may give some readers pause. It contradicts the assumption about Willie Mae's sexuality based on her gender resistance. But much of the music Willie Mae left behind is centered on the desire for and frustration with men, and she sang such lyrics with conviction, regardless of whether the lyrical subject was true for her.

Walker's choices are consistent with the intentional absurdity found in blues lyrics and literature. True to the classic blueswomen tradition, Willie Mae's lyrical leanings found her pleasantly and playfully antagonistic toward partners and potential suitors who were men. Additionally, Walker made Gracie Mae a grandmother — a Big Momma in the Black traditional Geneva Smitherman sense. I used this aspect of the story as an opportunity to think about Willie Mae's real-life son, who was taken by the state and not remembered by history. I do not believe that Walker, a woman who describes herself as queer, created this (seemingly) heterosexual context to distance Willie Mae from the possibility of being lesbian. Instead, I think, similarly to Willie Mae, that Walker uses her craft to tease readers and world-build around the range of emotions and possibilities.

The story takes place between 1955 and 1977, marking multiple transitional periods in Willie Mae's life. It also covers the entirety of Presley's career. We meet Gracie Mae Still in an unnamed/unknown southern Black town, inside her home with her "foots up" in her partner JT's lap, watching a baseball game. She notices two white men driving slowly past her house. As the two men park and make their way toward her home, Gracie Mae, with suspicion, opens the door. By this time, JT retreats to the bedroom to avoid the usual trouble that white men bring. The older man introduces himself as "the deacon" and his young companion as Traynor. When the deacon speaks, Gracie Mae hears a "hearty Southern way that makes my eyeballs ache," drawing a distinction between white southern English and Black southern English and the violence that lives in the gap between the two. Gracie Mae's attention to language highlights Willie Mae Thornton's mastery of Black English and how her strategic diction reveals her gift of chopping and screwing words to suit her sentences and their meanings. Like how she says "houn dawg" instead of "hound dog," or how she broke into stories between songs requiring her audience to respond to her Black-vernacular-based calls of "Y'all know what I'm talkin' 'bout?"

In their initial meeting, Gracie describes Traynor as "five feet nine, sort of womanish looking with real dark white skin and a red pouting mouth. His hair is black and curly, and he looks like a Louisiana Creole." *Dark white skin.* It is a fact that Presley's maternal great-great-great grandmother was a Cherokee woman named Morning White Dove, which, technically, makes Presley mixed race. The deacon could represent two people: Elvis's first manager, Sam Phillips, from Sun Records, and his manager from then out, Colonel Tom Parker, a Dutch man who in 1955 purchased Presley's contract from Sun Records with RCA's support.

The deacon's character shows that Traynor was groomed to be the face for a new genre of entertainment — white-faced soul. *Dark white skin.* To assure Gracie Mae that she was in good company, the deacon shared that "the boy learned to sing and dance livin' round you people out in the country. Practically cut his teeth on you." The deacon has come to Gracie Mae's door to persuade her to sell her famous song for $500 and all the copies she has of it in the house for another $500, for Traynor's use. It's true. Elvis was raised in Tupelo, Mississippi, and spent much of his time across the tracks from his segregated white community. He was drawn to the sounds coming from Shakerag, Tupelo's historically Black unincorporated community that helped lay the foundation for the Delta blues. In a June 27, 1956 interview with the *Charlotte Observer*, Presley spoke directly to this foundation: "The colored folks been singing it and playing it just like I'm doin' now, man, for more years than I know. They played it like that in the shanties and jook joints, and nobody paid it no mind 'til I goose it up. I got it from them. Down in Tupelo, Mississippi, I used to hear old Arthur Crudup bang his box the way I do now, and I said if I ever got to the place, I could feel all old Arthur felt, I'd be a music man like nobody ever saw."

Gracie Mae describes the deacon as an "older gentlemen dressed like a deacon. . . . He is maybe sixty, with white hair and beard, white silk shirt, black linen suit, black tie, and black shoes." I do not think of Colonel Parker, who is almost always photographed with a clean-shaven face. Instead, I think of the sometimes clean shaven but more often bearded Sam Phillips from Alabama, who "discovered" Elvis in Memphis. Sam Phillips grew up with a Black sharecropper he called Uncle Silas Payne, a man taken in by the Phillips family when he began losing his sight. I can neither imagine nor fully trust the conditions for this arrangement, but it somehow led to Phillips being honored among the many white men deemed founders or fathers of rock 'n' roll music. In the documentary *Sam Phillips: The Man Who Invented Rock 'n' Roll* (more inventions and white boy magic), Phillips says that Payne taught him "how to live and how to be happy and that no matter what came along, even when you're feeling bad, you're feeling good," which is to say, Silas Payne taught him that embedded in the blues are complex emotions, social critique, and stylized joy — misery resistance. This knowledge forms the basis for Willie Mae's "Laugh, Laugh, Laugh," in which she laughs between lyrics on beat. She then instructs listeners to "Keep on laughing all the time, man / Leave your worries behind / You'll end up so happy / With great peace of mind." The song has a big band, R&B swing to it, which not only satisfies her genre promiscuity but makes sense for the year it was recorded: 1956. Sam Phillips took to Memphis his understanding of this "blues epistemology," as Clyde Woods calls it, and his intimacy with the sounds of Blackness. Willie Mae and Silas Payne lived the blues and spread the gospel of survival within their respective communities.

As the deacon and Traynor make themselves comfortable in Gracie Mae's home, they offer her $500 for the song they've come to collect. The exact amount of the one-time payment Willie Mae received from Don Robey for recording "Hound Dog." Rebelliously, Alice never references anyone other than Gracie Mae as the owner of the song. With the stroke of her pen, Jerry Leiber, Mike Stoller, Johnny Otis, and Don Robey are removed from history. Through this fictional account, readers experience "Hound Dog" as the sole creation of Gracie Mae/Willie Mae and witness the Traynor/Elvis camp having to seek her permission to perform it. Elvis Presley never sought Willie Mae's permission, nor did he have to. Presley didn't have to seek permission to record Arthur Crudup's "That's All Right Mama" in 1954 for Sun Records either. Yet, shortly after Presley's recording, Arthur Crudup left the industry because he was cheated out of the royalties from the song that gave Elvis wings. The words he shares in David Szat-mary's *Rockin' in Time* before a lengthy recording hiatus are telling: "I realized I was making everybody rich, and here I was poor." After unsuccessful legal battles against the Elvis camp, Crudup died penniless. Walker enacts jus-tice on the page for Gracie Mae and others harmed by the racialized and gendered violence that defined the 1950s music publishing business.

Willie Mae (indirectly) and all the bluesmen Sam Phil-lips recorded — including B. B. King, Howlin' Wolf, and Ike Turner — helped build the reputation and the initial profits for Sun Records. With the success of "That's All Right, Mama" and the consistent radio play it received from Memphis DJ Dewey Phillips (no relation to Sam), Sun Records was officially a force in the industry. Rosco Gordon, the R&B artist who found an audience in Jamaica and whose sound was one of the musical influences that gave way to ska, was also on Sun Records. Meanwhile, it has been said by childhood friends and biographers that Elvis was an avid listener to the Memphis's Black radio station WDIA, which regularly played the music of Willie Mae Thornton.

It's fair to say that Memphis is a sacred space for Black music. The fact that Aretha took her first breath there gives us a clue. King's last breath tells us even more. Dias-porically, the island of Jamaica had its ear to the Memphis streets too. Willie Mae's connection to Memphis through the Peacock and Duke Records merger placed her on the national stage. Memphis is an entry point to Elvis and Wil-lie Mae's interrelated histories. Rufus Thomas's answer song to Willie Mae's "Hound Dog," "Bear Cat" (conceived by Sam Phillips), was Sun Record's first chart hit. I return to this point because Willie Mae's "Hound Dog" was not only the biggest song for Peacock Records but also marked the beginning of Sun Records as a bona fide hitmaker that attracted Elvis. Thomas was frank about what Elvis's success meant for his Black Sun Records labelmates. After Phillips signed Elvis, young white talent started flocking to Phillips's door. And when that happened, Rufus Thomas, in an interview held by the Smithsonian's Memphis Rock 'n' Soul Museum archives, observed "When Sam Phillips started working with Elvis, he discarded all of his black talent, including me." Johnny Cash, Carl Perkins, Jerry Lee Lewis, and Roy Orbison were among those white artists who found their way to Sun Records.

Alice Walker made artistic choices to change this story with ingenious character development. She introduced Gracie Mae Still to readers as someone who no longer performed, even though Willie Mae was on stage from 1940 until she died in 1984. In 1955, Willie Mae was recovering from the death of her friend Johnny Ace and hustling to make ends meet. She was locked into a fruitless contract with Peacock and back on the Chitlin' Circuit doing what Gracie Mae in the story describes as singing in "one little low-life jook after another, making ten dollars a night for myself if I was lucky, and sometimes bringing home nothing but my life." Walker gives us a blueswoman resting at home, though Willie Mae spent most of her career gigging from city to city, living with friends or staying in hotel/motel rooms and boarding houses. She even saw the inside of a few jail cells. Her music reflects the truth of her lived experience. Her lyrics in the song "Hard Times" though they may be fictional, function like testimony: "This little money that I'm making / I can't pull this heavy load /

Bill collectors coming to my home / Times getting hard in the city / I'm going down the road." In an interview, Willie Mae explained her understanding of the blues to Studs Terkel: "Well, when you been blue all your life, you got to know what it's all about, that ain't only on stage. Sometimes I didn't have nothing to eat, even soda crackers taste like cheese and cake."

Though he grew up poor, Elvis never worried about his next meal again once he found Sun Records. His success made it clear to Sam Phillips that change was inevitable. In the documentary *Sam Phillips: The Man Who Invented Rock 'n' Roll*, Phillips told his Sun Records secretary Marion Keisker, "The only way to get the music to a broader audience was to find a white boy with a Negro sound and more importantly, a Negro feel. I could make a billion dollars." Toward that end, he had Elvis record blues or R&B on one side of the record and country or rockabilly on the other. Most of the rockabilly audience was southern, working-class, cotton-picking and sharecropping white folk who grew up in the Pentecostal church. Elvis was the bridge. This criticism of Elvis is not to deny his talent. In "Nineteen Fifty-Five," Gracie Mae acknowledges that Traynor "wasn't doing too bad with my song either." Instead, the criticism is about what happened to Black musicians in the wake of Elvis being crowned king. Two years after Traynor records Gracie Mae's song, he returns to her home to express gratitude. When her grandchildren announce his arrival, they say, "Little Mama, Little Mama, it's that white man who sings ———— ———— ————." Acknowledging the fever around his cover, Gracie Mae says, "The children didn't call it my song anymore. Nobody did."

In "Nineteen Fifty-Five," Gracie Mae and Traynor are bonded by naïveté. By this time in the story, Traynor begins the pattern of visiting Gracie Mae and offering exquisite gifts (homes, farms, cars) of appreciation. He also uses the visits to confess his trouble with success. He has become aware of what he reads as the inauthentic celebration of his work and complains about his distance from the material. "I done sung the song it seems like a million times this year," he says. "I've sung it, and I've sung it, and I'm making forty thousand dollars a day offa it, and you know what, I don't have the faintest notion of what the song means." Gracie Mae now realizes the mistake she made with the original deal: "These suckas is making forty-thousand a day offa my song and now they gonna come back and try to swindle me out of the original thousand." She also knew he had become more famous for the song than she ever would have. Traynor is in too deep, and Gracie Mae begins to live with the ghost of her decision.

Gracie Mae is additionally frustrated by the fact that Traynor is doing much more than covering the song; he's also using her intonation, ad-libs, and moves. "Well, Lord have mercy, I said listening to him. If I'da closed my eyes, it could have been me. He had followed every turning of my voice, side streets, avenues, red lights, train crossings and all. It gives me a chill." Jack Halberstam exposes Elvis's version of "Hound Dog" as being more sinister than a cover: "What Elvis takes from Thornton, however, is more than the song, more than the raw material. He takes the shout from Thornton, the defiance, the confident rejection of the 'high-class poseur.' He takes her confidence, her rhythm, her phrasing even, and her gender mobility." Elvis studied and copied others, too. "Don't Be Cruel" songwriter Otis Blackwell confirmed in a 1984 interview with David Letterman that Elvis relied on the demo tapes he provided him with to learn how to sing Blackwell's songs. He also revealed that part of his songwriting deal with RCA required sharing cowriting credit with Presley, regardless of the latter's nonexistent contribution. White covers of Black music are costly, and as Traynor asks Gracie Mae every chance he gets, what good do the songs do when you don't know their meaning? The lesson Walker makes plain is this: you can twist and shout, but you can't imitate a life lived.

I'm not sure of how much control Willie Mae had over the years in selecting songs to perform, but she boldly applied her signature to each tune. On most songs, Willie Mae freestyles during the bridge, either breaking from the song's theme to encourage musicians during solos or animating themes by employing vocal antics like barking on "Hound Dog" or crowing on "Little Red Rooster." She also created a brand around the term "hound dog" and used the phrase on multiple songs just to flex her ownership. For example, in "Just Like a Dog (Barking Up the Wrong Tree)," she throws in "Just like an old houn' dawg / Barking up the wrong tree." She also mashed up "Wade in the Water" by adding "hound dog in the water" during the chorus. Unlike Elvis, Willie Mae was a songwriter and multitalented force who woke up to the blues and crafted them to her listeners' liking. She wrote most of the material on her albums and was particularly prolific as a songwriter throughout the sixties. The problem is, it's difficult to trace her catalog as a songwriter because of the industry's publishing schemes. What we do know is that she wrote "Ball 'n' Chain," which catapulted Janis Joplin into the position of "queen of rock." This speaks to both the power of Willie Mae's words and the nature of white-faced music supremacy. She had talent, experience, and a legit brand in "Hound Dog," but she was a big woman and America has a long history "mammifying" Black bodies such as hers. Her weight, coupled with her masculine appearance, almost guaranteed that the music industry would find a feminine white woman to sell in her place.

There are many references to weight in "Nineteen Fifty-Five." Gracie Mae talks about losing weight, gaining it, and losing it again. She finds an unlikely connection between herself and Traynor. When she sees him during their now regular visits, her inner dialogue lets us into how she sees the weight: "He's getting fat for sure, but he's still slim compared to me. I'll never see three hundred pounds again, and I've just about said (excuse me) fuck it." In several Willie Mae Thornton songs she refers to her weight and, very specifically, the figure of three hundred pounds. In "They Call Me Big Mama," the opening lines are "Well they call me Big Mama / 'Cause I weigh three hundred pounds." This recording for Peacock communicates the struggle the label had promoting her work and its reliance on cliché references to her size to push a record forward. In the song "Stop A-Hoppin' on Me," she exclaims again, "They call me Big Mama / Know I'm big and fat / But what you don't know / I'm tight like that."

Willie Mae struggled with weight all her life: from being teased as a child to being taken less seriously artistically as an adult. She was painfully aware of how reviews of her performances almost always connected her musical prowess to her weight and height. Alice Walker works the story to get to the essence of Gracie Mae and Traynor's struggles with their bodies. With a more profound reflection on her health, Gracie Mae admits, "I finally faced up to the fact that my fat is the hurt I don't admit, not even to myself, and that I been trying to bury it from the day I was born." Traynor confides in Gracie Mae that eating helps him deal with the emptiness in his life. She notices that the more popular he becomes, the more distant he grows from his own body. When she visits him around this time, she notes that he slurs and has "nothing behind his eyes."

By the 1970s, Traynor was well established, having produced multiple albums and films and performed worldwide, but something was amiss. He was overweight, wealthy, lonely, and struggling with addiction. During another visit, Gracie Mae noticed that while the two shared a meal, Traynor ate chicken, pork chops, and chitlins in one sitting. Indeed, some believe that soul food contributed to the decline and eventually the death of Presley.

On a surface level, "Nineteen Fifty-Five" calls attention to centuries of emotional labor performed by Black women, even at their own expense. But it also made me think about the emotional labor that white artists perform when their fame and wealth are dependent on Black creativity. Presley gets exposed as a shell of a character, tortured by the perils of his dependence on Blackness. "Couldn't be anything worse than being famous the world over for something you don't even understand," says Gracie Mae. The friendship Alice creates between Gracie Mae and Traynor is not unreasonable. After all, Presley's public and private relationships with Black women gave his fans a clue. From his backup singers, the Sweet Inspirations, to his long-term cook Mary Jenkins Langston (whom he showered with gifts), to his maid Nancy Rooks, Elvis was mothered by Black women — personally and musically. What Alice does with "Nineteen Fifty-Five" prompts her readers to contend with the toll on the Black folk, women in particular, who are charged with keeping him alive until it's discovered that nothing can save him.

Traynor is haunted by the souls who have been buried nameless so that he can remain seen. Literarily, Gracie "Willie" Mae and Traynor "Elvis" Presley have been released from their narrative bondage, and Alice Walker uses "the beauty of the authentic" as a baseline for their story's reconfiguring. Traynor died in 1977, as did Elvis. When Gracie Mae talks about what the word is on the street following his death, she says, "Some said fat, some said heart, some said alcohol, some said drugs." Gracie Mae outlives Traynor. Willie Mae outlives Elvis. Gracie Mae and Willie Mae are not the ones to be pitied. They had something Elvis never had: the real meaning of, and therefore joy in creating, music based on lived experience.

I do not doubt that millions of Black Elvis fans exist worldwide. And I'm astonished by Walker's work to restore Gracie Mae's power in this matter, as well as the work she does to grant Traynor an inner life that transcends the cultural-theft narrative. In this way, Walker is very generous. However, there are still those who remain unimpressed by what Elvis and the character Traynor represent. In the same 1999 interview with Bob Costas discussed in a previous chapter, Ray Charles, sitting on the edge of his piano bench with a black coat and crisp white button-up shirt, said, "I guess I am going to lose at least about a third of my fans right now, but to say that Elvis was so great and so outstanding and like they say he's the king. Nah. I got in trouble because one guy asked me this question, and I said, the king of what? And he got mad at me. I don't think of Elvis like that because I know too many far greater artists. . . . I think all this stuff about them saying he's a king, that's a piece of bunk." Then, with his sunglasses swaying in soulful defiance, he says, "Sorry, next question. Don't ask me no more about Elvis."

CALIFORNIA LOVE / CALIFORNIA DREAMIN'

There is a saying among black Angelenos that all black folks live south of Pico Boulevard. While this is, of course, an exaggeration, south of Pico we can indeed find major black communities, from the core of Central Avenue to Watts and Compton south, to Leimert Park and Baldwin Hills to the west and north, areas where the more affluent were able to move with the fall of restrictive covenants. "South of Pico" is also a metaphor for African American migrations and the ancestral home of most black Angelenos.

KELLIE JONES

The Willie Mae Thornton of the 1960s sang from a different place in her gut. The fact that she produced fewer than ten songs between 1961 and 1964 says little about her growth as an artist. She excelled at prestigious festivals and venues and flourished between scarce recordings in the underground blues scene. Joining hundreds of thousands before her, Willie Mae took the Black migratory route between Texas and California. She stumbled into multiple movements with new musicians and circled back to collaborators who were part of her formative years. The artists she worked with during these years were Muddy Waters, James Cotton, and B. B. King. Willie Mae's life in the 1960s was full of masterful pivots and familiar pitfalls. From troubled business partnerships to jaw-dropping live shows, it was clear that she had again shifted into a new shape.

In 1961 Willie Mae stepped back into the studio for the Oakland-based, Black-owned Bay-Tone Records. The label, founded by Bradley Taylor, recorded both obscure and known artists between 1958 and 1963. Willie Mae was the most famous among them. Her partnership with Bay-Tone yielded a handful of songs such as "Big Mama's Blues" and "You Did Me Wrong." In the sessions and on wax, Willie Mae's voice is older — more cigarettes, more alcohol, more living. Wiser in the rhythm. On "You Did Me Wrong," her vocals are raw and artfully strained as though shouting through the 1950s catapulted her into a state of raspy grace. She's yelling into the mic and leading the backing band with seasoned confidence. "Big Mama's Blues" is a down-tempo instrumental composed by Thornton. The prominence of the harmonica in each piece is a signal that she will no longer push her instrument to the side for labels who want to limit her to singing, as Don Robey did.

From now on, Willie Mae would integrate her voice, the harmonica, and the drums (or any combination of those elements) and make them part of her cache of performance and recording tools. The singles attracted a slight buzz and earned her a write-up in *Billboard*. Journalists hailed her "return," but little came from it aside from a nod to her existence and her once-was status. This also speaks to how *Billboard* editors, most of them white since its inception in 1894, were able to determine her relevance. Narratives of her return focused on the chart-topping "Hound Dog" to the exclusion of nearly a decade of her subsequent work. The obscurity of a Black artist can be invented and retracted by white boy magic.

The year 1961 was pivotal for Willie Mae as a songwriter. She wrote and recorded a song for Bay-Tone that would one day change the course of her life, "Ball 'n' Chain." Reminiscent of Robey's decision to shelve "Hound Dog," Bradley stalled the official release of "Ball 'n' Chain." She signed a deal with the label that, again, led to questions around publishing and copyright issues. Within a year of the Bay-Tone releases, Willie Mae recorded for another Black-owned label, Irma Records. The label was founded by musician and producer Bob Geddins, a Black Texan who migrated to California and was known as the "Godfather of the East Bay Blues." Geddins also produced Willie Mae's good friend Jimmy McCracklin and saucy blueswoman Sugar Pie Desanto. Willie Mae recorded two songs for Irma. In "Don't Talk Back," her voice is deep, almost baritone, and brilliantly unrecognizable. She's flexing her range. And it's a song that echoes the late '50s ska sound of Jamaica in its emphasis on the afterbeat. For this number she uses the Hi-Tones vocal group as backup singers. In "Big Mama's Coming Home," her voice is sure and seems to leave the band behind, which scrambles to match her energy.

Willie Mae recorded for another Cali-based Black label, Sharp Records, headed by James C. Moore. Due to a legal dispute, the label was renamed Jasman Records. One song is a funked-up version of "Me and My Chauffeur," a twist on one of her favorite songs by Memphis Minnie, "Chauffeur Blues." She also recorded a tune called "Before Day," also known as "Big Mama's Blues." In fact, Willie Mae recorded "Big Mama's Blues" under several titles for several different labels, and Sharp leased the version she recorded for them to Los Angeles–based Kent Records around 1966. In contrast to her recorded work in the 1950s, she's listed as the writer for most of the songs recorded during this period (aside from the classics she covers). This is not to say that songwriting credit is equated to fair compensation. Her Bay-Tone recording of "You Did Me Wrong" points to a reckless lover, but one can't help but think of it as a theme song to her experience as an artist in the dirty blues.

In a rare interview with the *Fifth Estate*, a Michigan newspaper, one unidentified writer covered Willie Mae's status as an artist in the late 1960s. In a refreshing change from mainstream media, the writer speaks to the exploitation Willie Mae had experienced: "There are in fact, a good many records produced for various labels . . . for which Big Mama has received little or nothing." When the writer asked Willie Mae about her business affairs, she responded sharply, "Don't ask me how the business works, I'd like to know that myself; when I figure it out, I'll let you know." Her answer may explain the label hopping and the number of managers she went through while living in California. Michael Spörke suggests that a string of predatorial industry insiders sought her out *because* of her limited understanding of the business: "There were all kinds of managers that wanted to grab her, and for a person who could not read or write properly, it's an easy thing to get cheated." Many of the great blues folk and our great-grandparents were functionally illiterate, and that legacy of slavery served and helped build the wealth of the American music industry.

The music business, like sharecropping, was designed to exploit anyone unaware of the legal loopholes. So, it wasn't just that Willie Mae was illiterate and therefore vulnerable to mismanagement. She and many other musicians had to make decisions to ensure immediate access to food, clothing, and shelter. Such choices eliminated for artists the possibility of securing generational wealth. Paying the families of exploited blues artists alone makes sense for any kind of reparations initiative. This is evidenced by the sheer number of lawyers who waged a legal battle with music corporations in the hopes of recouping decades of monetary loss and penned copyright cases against white musicians like Elvis Presley, Eric Clapton, and Rod Stewart.

In nearly all of those cases, Black musicians who demanded their fair share of the resources generated from contributions they had made to an artist, song, or production, were rejected in favor of the better-resourced white musicians. More sinister is how several of the aforementioned white artists used their platforms (on stage, in interviews, and in their memoirs) to talk about Black blues originators to whom they are indebted. Willie Mae's experience in the industry is complicated. Most of her exploiters were Black men who crafted their business models based on the successful exploitive practices of white men.

In 1961 Willie Mae played regularly in Alameda County's Russell City. The small community was a destination point for Black people migrating from the South, Latino braceros, and shipyard workers who came in large numbers after World War II. Russell City's nightlife scene was known among Black musicians nationally as a place to jam with the house band or play for highly participatory audiences. Several famous artists stopped in Russell City after playing in San Francisco and Oakland venues to experience its club life. Willie Mae played Friday and Saturday nights at Russell City's best-known venue, the Country Club. It was here that legends like Etta James and Ray Charles made surprise appearances. It is also true that she and her teenage pianist Billy Dunn were arrested at the Country Club after the two fought on stage (Dunn was arrested for the fight, and when Willie Mae tried to stop the cops from arresting him, she was booked too). They spent a few hours in jail but were released and eventually made it to his mother's house. When they arrived, Willie Mae cooked Billy Dunn a no-hard-feelings meal.

Sadly, the arrest set off a series of hardships. Willie Mae was fired from the Country Club because of her probation status from previous altercations at the time of her arrest. She was also fired from a Beachcomber gig in Santa Cruz. Tragically, between 1963 and 1964, the City of Hayward incorporated the ground on which Russell City was located. Hayward officials displaced, bulldozed, and tore down the community (making sure to get rid of any traces of Black and Brown cultural life) to build an industrial park. Still alive and leading the Russell City Memorial Blues Band, Billy Dunn, now seventy-eight, joked about Willie Mae in the 2010 documentary film *The Russell City Blues*: "She was an excellent drummer, and she could fight too." This moment in Willie Mae's life resonates with me. Growing up in Cali I was suspended and held in detention for fighting for my rights too. Even when the rights that had been violated were in my mind. I learned early that reputation matters and hot heads are liabilities. The costs of those lessons—be they financial in Willie Mae's case, or social in my case (when I was prevented from going on certain school field trips)—have lasting consequences. Her life through this literary journey remains a teacher—or more accurately, a mirror. Knowing when not to fight and distinguishing friend from foe is key.

One common, if misguided, narrative about the blues is that by the 1960s they had become less relevant and needed a revival. The shifting interest in blues was part of how young, white, well-resourced festival producers and venue promoters created a lucrative market around the idea of saving the music. Unfortunately, the idea of saving the music led many to position themselves as its paternalistic owners, curators, and gatekeepers. But were the blues truly fading in relevance? I can't be sure about Black private listening practices and the intimate connection that defines what Black people collectively kept in rotation in the 1950s and 1960s. However, I do know that Willie Mae's informal artist residency in the historically Black unincorporated town of Russell City matters. It reframes the conversation from being held under the umbrella of declining interest in the blues to one that centers the continuation of Black cultural production in underground spaces and modern jook joints—away from the reach of white saviors. Willie Mae, as usual, put it frankly in her interview with the *Fifth Estate* journalist: "The blues ain't never died for me."

While rock 'n' roll was emerging from the gut of Black American blues, Willie Mae was holding down one-off shows and weekly gigs in the Bay Area. She traveled by car with her drum kit and performed at places like the Basin Street West in San Francisco and the Rhumboogie in Oakland, shouting over rhythm sections and premiering songs she had written for Black audiences. Rock 'n' roll was thriving and yet hostile toward its Black creators. Maureen Mahon calls attention to this hostility, asserting that "even after young white artists began appropriating and popularizing black musical sound, the majority of African-American artists still had minimal access to the charts and radio airplay, limiting their ability to capitalize on the music trends they had fostered."

An example of this appropriation and popularization of blues sound is the Rolling Stones, who played their first gig at the Marquee Club in London in 1962. Within two years, they recorded two albums (*The Rolling Stones [England's Newest Hitmakers]* and *12 × 5*). By 1965 they had reached their "height of fame" period as one of the most popular transatlantic bands. Maybe this is why Willie Mae famously stated that "rock 'n' roll was nuthin' but the blues speeded up." Still, groups like the Rolling Stones were supplied with cars, mansions, and expanding accounts from touring and album sales, while Willie Mae was living in the Eddy Hotel and Motel on Eddy Street in San Francisco. In contrast to Jimmy McCracklin's observation that "in those days nobody was making big money like they make now," Elvis Presley and the Sun Records white family of rockabilly rockers were making gratuitous sums of money and living in excess off the blues. Elvis Presley purchased the grounds for Graceland around 1957, and by the 1960s he had built an empire. The Graceland estate, where Elvis is buried today, remains the most visited and profitable gravesite in the United States today.

Willie Mae's life took another turn when two Britons by the name of Paul and Valerie Oliver traveled to the United States with the support of the BBC. The result of that trip was a record and book released in 1965 under the same title, *Conversations with the Blues*. Four years later, Paul Oliver released another book. After taking a trip through the American South in 1964 interviewing and recording blues singers, Oliver wrote *The Story of the Blues*. He also wrote one of the many biographies on Bessie Smith. Oliver was one of the key players in the "blues revival," and there is no doubt that he generated income from these projects; to a far lesser degree, Willie Mae benefited in the form of increased attention and opportunities.

Chris Strachwitz, a German Berkley-based blues enthusiast, accompanied the Olivers for part of their trip and recorded one of the most often-cited interviews in Willie Mae's history. He had seen her perform in Santa Cruz and knew he wanted to add her to his roster of artists for independent label Arhoolie Records. In the interview she was funny, still influenced by her professional training in comedy. She laughed at the response to hearing "Hound Dog" playing at a Dayton, Ohio, venue where she performed: "So I goes up in the operating room, I said, you mind playing that again 'cause I hadn't heard the record in so long I had forgot the words myself." Her comedic timing was on display, and I imagine her being an exemplary opponent in a contest shooting the dozens. She was playful, witty, and protectively hardened. "'Hound Dog' just took off like a jet," she said with a soulful but snarky tone. After the statement, she offered a few seconds of laughter, like a punctuation that summed up years of recognizing her own value even when the industry didn't. Though the interview was incredibly personal, Willie Mae maintained and cultivated mystique. Black privacy. Her generosity, even when she declined to share her age, speaks to where she was at the time—in the midst of another transition, looking for work.

When Strachwitz asked her if there was anything she wanted to tell the people listening, she answered, "Yeah, I need a job, I need a job. Help, help!" And when referencing the success of "Hound Dog" compared to her other songs that barely charted, she said, "I need another 'Hound Dog,' or a cat or somethin'"—again in true Black English form, disappearing her *g*. What stands out to me about this interview is Willie Mae's vulnerability and the power dynamic between her and Strachwitz. I'm uncomfortable with the fact that Paul Oliver and Chris Strachwitz have the financial might to change the course of her life (some of it earned from their respective "interests" in Black music), and that their curiosity about the blues is linked to her fate. What does it mean for her to sit in front of the camera or speak into a recorder and use the opportunity to seek employment even though she'd been performing at that point for over twenty years? All these contradictions led to decisions she made that worked against her own interests. When it wasn't white men figuring out how to get as much from her as possible, it was Black men replicating their behavior. While she was often hamstrung by poor representation, some of those managers made incredible contributions to her career.

Willie Mae met James C. Moore in 1964 when they ran into each other in a hotel where she was staying in Richmond, California, twenty minutes north of Oakland. Acting on a cue from several people in the industry who suggested they work together, Moore approached Willie

Mae about management. Before he did this, though, he consulted with one of his good friends, the jazz artist Cannonball Adderley, who advised him to "sign her tomorrow." Indeed, he did. Within weeks, she was recording and booked at prominent festivals. Under Moore's management, Willie Mae performed in front of folk, rock, jazz, and blues audiences both domestically and internationally. The most famous of her appearances was at the 1964 Monterey Jazz Festival. That year she shared the stage with jazz greats like Herbie Hancock, Wayne Shorter, the Dizzy Gillespie Quintet, Ron Carter, and the Miles Davis Quintet. Spörke notes that Miles asked Willie Mae to accompany him with her harmonica for a song, though we don't know whether she accepted the invitation. Her set list for the show reinforced her connection to spirituals: she performed "Steal Away," "Old Time Religion," "Down by the Riverside," and of course "Hound Dog."

Willie Mae made such an impression at the Monterey festival that she returned in 1966 and 1968. This new shape that Willie Mae took positioned her close to jazz musicians, who respected her music and her skilled ear. In fact, her performance at the festival sparked a potential collaboration that was never realized. Duke Ellington reached out to James Moore requesting a conversation to discuss working together. When Moore shared the news with Willie Mae and encouraged her to call, she refused for unexplained reasons. Moore and Spörke attributed this to her general shyness and her artistic insecurities. Still, later that year, she went on to play the jazz workshop in Boston with Muddy Waters, Louis Jordan, and, again, Miles Davis. The first half of the 1960s teach us that Willie Mae's life was more than a story of financial struggles and personal trauma. The money stolen from her and the work she did to earn a living by no means reflects a failed career. Willie Mae moved to Los Angeles in 1964 and stayed with her people until she got settled. The rest of the 1960s proved that she had become a fully realized artist and southern ambassador summoned to take the blues across the Atlantic.

WILLIE MAE INNA ENGLAND

I have walked into the palaces of kings and queens and into the houses of presidents. And much more. But I could not walk into a hotel in America and get a cup of coffee, and that made me mad.

JOSEPHINE BAKER

Life in Paris was to some extent protected by the fact that I carried a green passport. This passport proclaimed that I was a free citizen of a free country, and was not, therefore, to be treated as one of Europe's uncivilized, black possessions. This same passport, on the other side of the ocean, underwent a sea change and proclaimed that I was not an African prince, but a domestic nigger and that no foreign government would be offended if my corpse were to be found clogging up the sewers.

JAMES BALDWIN

In 1951, James Baldwin's lover brought him to the Swiss Alps to escape the noise of Paris and sink deeper into his writing. In his rereading of Baldwin's essay "Stranger in the Village" in 2014, Teju Cole wrote in the *New Yorker* that "Baldwin had to bring his records with him in the fifties, like a secret stash of medicine." In his secret stash you could find Bettye Swann and Billie Holiday — artists who kept him company, along with his lover, as he wrote his first novel, *Go Tell It on the Mountain*.

In Baldwin's 1959 essay "The Discovery of What it Means to Be American," he shares, "I'd never listened to Bessie Smith in America (in the same way that, for years, I would not touch watermelon), but in Europe she helped to reconcile me to being a 'nigger.'" It was Bessie Smith, he said, who "helped me to dig back to the way I myself must have spoken when I was a pickaninny, and to remember the things I had heard and seen and felt. I had buried them very deep."

Nearly seventy years later, I'm writing from my North London studio contemplating this combination of worlds — Baldwin, the blues, the Black south, and Europe. Like Baldwin, I traveled to Europe with a bag of records, heavy enough to handle but light enough to move. Keen selections. We both crossed the Atlantic with eyes set on a second home. A home away from the limitations of how Blackness was/is imagined in America. In Europe, Baldwin and I discovered that we could have a different relationship with the blues — partly because of the distance from the social conditions that produced them. While he immersed himself into the "cadence" he described in Bessie Smith's voice, I focused on the personality and musicianship that emerged from Willie Mae's southern roots.

In 1965, Willie Mae traveled from the Chitlin' Circuit to the royal concert halls for a European tour with the American Folk Blues Festival. The annual tour was founded by the German musician, concert promoter, and writer Horst

Lippman and Fritz Rau, an influential German tastemaker and concert promoter known for his efforts to introduce jazz and blues to Europe in the '50s and '60s. Together they created the concert promotion team known as Lippman + Rau and organized the first American Folk Blues Festival in 1962. Wille Mae performed on the tour in major cities in Switzerland, Germany, Denmark, Netherlands, France, Spain, Belgium, and the UK.

The 1965 American Folk Blues Festival cohort—Willie Mae Thornton, Buddy Guy, Big Walter "Shaky" Horton, J. B. Lenoir, Eddie Boyd, Doctor Ross, Jimmy Lee, John Lee Hooker, Roosevelt Sykes, and Mississippi Fred McDowell—were impressed by their upscale hotels and the prestigious venues where they performed. This is what America does to Black people. It sets the bar so low that when you venture elsewhere and get treated like a human being, even the basics—that is to say, the benefits typically reserved for white artists of similar stature—become a luxury. Imagine traveling far beyond the Alabama Slave Laws and landing in London to blow the harmonica and sing.

Willie Mae's time in Europe must have opened her eyes even more to the finicky response to the blues by a trend-chasing American music industry. She felt courted and catered to in this foreign place, as did many other artists. Testimonies from Alberta Hunter, Josephine Baker, Richard Wright, and Nina Simone tell us that they experienced better treatment—less violence, higher pay—for their work in the Black American arts while in Europe. James Baldwin, however, reminds us that white supremacy and colonialism had begun, developed, and evolved in Europe over the centuries and that the UK was an especially brutal colonial force.

Back in the United States, while blues artists' opportunities to make a living were fading, the music was not. Between 1960 and 1965, soul had become the primary sonic voice for Black people. Performing the blues in Europe was a way for artists to keep the genre alive in the public eye and capitalize on its growing international relevance. That didn't stop Willie Mae from noticing familiar racialized patterns. Though her time in Europe was short-lived, she was there long enough to notice the absence of Black Europeans in the audience. Likewise, she saw their absence among the festival's production team and the pool of local musicians.

Lippman + Rau played to stereotypes in presenting American blues people to European audiences. The set design created for the performers was reminiscent of the rural south portrayed in all-Black musicals like *Cabin in the Sky* (1943). And though there were rocking chairs and mock porches, the audience missed call-and-response cues and the highly interactive relationship between audience and performer, which speak to where the blues are from. Europeans listened quietly, sometimes confusing the artists. Taking without giving. *Eating the other*, as bell hooks might say.

The cultural distance between Black American performers and European audiences was daunting for Willie Mae and her associates. They were aware of how the othering of Black people was something to be expected wherever they landed and Europe was no exception. Knowing they had been chosen as ambassadors on this sometimes-lonely journey, Willie Mae and her co-performers dressed formally for the occasion — conks, ties, and crisp white shirts. The women who performed with the festival (after the inaugural cohort) wore gowns and dresses. Willie Mae performed in a long gown or her famous long skirt, plaid flannel shirt, and matching Kangol-style fishing hat. Her dangling earrings traveled across the Atlantic with her too. Between shows, Willie Mae, influenced by southwestern fashion sensibilities, traveled in her "real clothes," which consisted of cowboy boots, jeans, and big-brimmed hats. Stylish on her own terms off the clock.

During one of the filmed performances, Willie Mae was introduced by a suave Buddy Guy. Upon hearing her name, she strutted out from stage left, singing without a microphone, making herself heard before she was seen. The bop she walked with warranted a head nod in any US Black city. Black cool was a crucial part of her performance. However, there were other details about her show that inspired questions or activated my imagination. Willie Mae, to my surprise, was carrying a large floral pocketbook when she walked out on stage. It looked out of place in her hands, as if the stage manager tossed it to her just before the show began. While moaning and hollering the first few notes of the song, she sat the pocketbook on top of a set of crates on stage before finding her sweet spot close to the musicians. I watched and wondered if the pocketbook, too, were a prop.

Willie Mae's first audible words that day were "I just want to let everybody know all about it," which by then had become her signature introduction to set the record straight for the song she knew everyone wanted to hear, "Hound Dog." She danced with the tune, owning it even more now that it was over a decade old. Buddy, meanwhile, was picking and bending strings over Fred Below's funky drumming. Willie Mae summoned her musical family to the stage for the following number and shouted out their names as though assembling a small army. Then, with J. B. Lenoir, Shaky Horton, Doc Ross, and John Lee Hooker on stage, she announced, in the spirit of a conductor preparing the crowd for the festival finale, "We all gotta a little thing and we call it the 'Down Home Shakedown.'" From there, she broke into a harmonica solo until the next performer joined for their turn. A ring shout on the road.

Despite their quiet attention, the audience witnessed a world-class blues cipher—like a freestyle rap circle where every emcee steps forward for a chance to shine. The blues cipher in Europe that night was led by a highly spirited woman from Alabama. The artists she invited to the stage watched for her approval, and she permitted them to enter the circle with handclaps and eye signals. She brought a sophisticated southern call-and-response system to Europe. Willie Mae also created the space to showcase the importance of the harmonica in the blues, and the trained ear might hear the regional distinctions that determined how it was played. Under her guidance, the musicians' collective sound was a teacher, and she was the perfect hype person for the group. During solos, she called the musician's name and told them to get it, right as they were getting it.

Watching archival footage of the American Folk Blues Festival, you get the feeling that maybe Europeans are interested in the interior worlds of blues people, even if the set design relied on unimaginative associations and the audience sits quietly as passive consumers. That maybe, even when silent, they had a sense of curiosity. Such curiosity was met with an educative component organized by the festival producers. Between performances for the

1969 festival, for example, Chris Strachwitz followed several acts on stage to share a short bio. He then explained where the musician was from and described the style of blues they represented. Thus, the American Folk Blues Festival allowed Europeans to hear a range of music from the Black American diaspora — from the Mississippi Delta blues to Chicago electric blues, from Texas R&B to Louisiana zydeco.

This appreciation for the blues took place as Black folk back home worked to maintain their dignity under the violent American political regime. In March 1965, Martin Luther King and about six hundred fellow freedom fighters walked the Edmund Pettus Bridge in Willie Mae's home state of Alabama to demand voting rights. During the march, protestors were attacked with whips, billy clubs, and tear gas by state troopers. They were kicked and spat on by a local white mob. The violence, captured on television for a global audience, became known as "Bloody Sunday." Not to be confused with the "Bloody Sunday" massacre that occurred when British soldiers shot twenty-six unarmed civilians in Ireland in 1972, but it was the same energy.

Malcolm X, with his street charm and political fire, fueled a new line of questioning from youth organizers who were no longer convinced that nonviolence and civil disobedience should be primary strategies for Black liberation. Malcolm's graceful anger and critical reading of white supremacy, not to mention his willingness to mobilize Black people around the idea of self-defense, was heralded by organizers such as Stokely Carmichael (Kwame Touré). But in February 1965, the same year Willie Mae landed in Europe, Malcolm X was assassinated. And while that was tragic and weighed heavy on the collective heart, there was balm — organizers suffered the blow dealt by Malcolm's murder, but they also thrived in the fight as soul music had become part of the movement.

In the spirit of field work and plantation songs that used lyrics to organize rebellion, Black music played a key role in describing the condition of Black America. Soul music in the age of Black Power became a unique call to action. Emily J. Lordi theorizes soul music as the sound of Black resilience and claims that the struggle that yielded this sound is "the logic of soul." "That logic," she says, "shaped a cultural sensibility that was bigger than soul music but that was especially audible in the music due to the commentary that shaped its social life." The arts in general provided an opportunity to engage, mobilize, and inspire, and the Black Arts Movement that emerged in 1965 was no different.

A collective of poets, jazz scholars, and community-based cultural critics, the Black Arts movement fashioned itself as a radical platform. Its affiliated artists created space to highlight the wealth discrepancy between Black jazz and blues artists and white promoters, journalists, and record company executives. Through a collective body of work, it articulated that white people were not only profiting from the music but also dictating how the music was contextualized and defined in literature, musicology, and various white-owned music publications.

Though Lippman + Rau and Chris Strachwitz were said to have treated the blues artists well, the glaring power imbalance was unmistakable at the American Folk Blues Festival. The festival was not exempt from participating in a global structure of stealing or profiting from the labor of Black artists while the artists themselves continued to be paid for one-off recordings and performances. Another concern is the fact that too many of the Black artists chosen to represent the genre/geography were men. Beyond the white reach for Black American folk and blues music, the festival promoters must account for their gendering— of the blues. The festival's gender politics were revealed by the sheer number of women who were *not* invited to perform. Those invited were expected to show up less as peers and more as exceptional singers— accessories to the "real blues instrumentalists." This might explain why only one woman was invited to perform per festival.

The American Folk Blues Festival ran from 1962 to 1970, paused for two years, and then tapered off for its final run in 1985. The first woman to perform at the festival was Helen Humes in 1962, and from there, Victoria Spivey in 1963; Sugar Pie Desanto in 1964; Willie Mae Thornton in 1965; Sippie Wallace in 1966; and Koko Taylor in 1967. Women were not invited to perform between 1968 and 1971. Only three women sang *and* played their instruments: Queen Sylvia Embry played her bass in 1983, Victoria Spivey played the ukulele, and Willie Mae Thornton blew the harmonica. Willie Mae Thornton was one of only two women who performed twice at the festival. After her 1965 performance, she returned with a new cohort in 1972. The other woman who performed twice was Margie Evans of Louisiana, who lit up the stage in 1981 and 1985. In 1981, Evans performed a rather impressive cover of "Hound Dog" while sporting a 1981 post-disco headband in the spirit of Miriam Makeba's South African cultural fashion accessory. Her version of "Hound Dog," faster in tempo, made clear that Willie Mae's signature song was still relevant to the blues in the 1980s. Though written by two white men, Willie Mae owned it, which meant it belonged to Black communities.

For Willie Mae, the American Folk Blues Festival was an all-star jam session but also an occasion to finally get the full album she deserved. The chance to record came about through another European, Arhoolie Records founder Chris Strachwitz. Strachwitz, whom I introduced in an earlier chapter, fell in love with Black musicians shortly after his family migrated from Germany to the Bay Area in 1947. He realized quickly that love for Black music could be lucrative for white men. His exchange with Willie Mae was lucrative too. Chris is often credited for revitalizing Willie Mae's career, and that's partly true. He played a role in getting her to Europe for the American Folk Blues Festival. And upon catching her live performances in Bay Area venues, he knew he wanted to produce a record with her.

The word "arhoolie" was used to describe field hands who shouted in song through forced labor, which is to say that Chris started an enterprise named after the musical responses to inhumane working conditions in hostile American fields in the South. In 1960, the field hands were but a generation away from the sharecropper plantation. Relatedly, Arhoolie's breakthrough as an independent label was made possible because of a Texan musician named Mance Lipscomb. Mance, a name given to him by a friend, was short for emancipation. The first LP Arhoolie released was Lipscomb's *Texas Sharecropper and Songster* in 1960. After its success, Chris continued his search for Black folk singers in the fields, on the streets of chocolate cities, and in Black rural communities. The musicians he "found" were financially vulnerable and therefore eager to agree to deals, no matter how exploitative. Folklorist as predator. Strachwitz was part of a long line of resourced and curious white magic men who showed up at churches, front porches, and convict leasing camps to record the sounds of blues people. Maybe that's why Alice Walker's short story "Nineteen Fifty-Five" begins with a white man on Gracie Mae's porch making her an offer for one of her songs.

As long as race and power remained a critical factor in how "business" was conducted regarding field recordings, the laborers who produced the blues were caught up in a cycle that Amiri Baraka described in his 1966 essay as "The Changing Same: (R&B and New Black Music)." The American music industry is bound up with legacies of slavery, and it mirrored elements of the carceral system to build its wealth and notoriety. So my question is not *did* Chris benefit from the labor of Willie Mae Thornton, but *how* did he benefit and, more, how will his family continue to reap the benefits from his encounter with Willie Mae? It's important to reiterate that Willie Mae Thornton died poor and is buried in an unmarked grave. A February 8, 1976, *New York Times* announcement of Mance Lipscomb's death gives us more clues. His obituary highlighted his struggle with poverty up until the end of his life: "Although he recorded several albums for a record company, Mr. Lipscomb earned little more than $1,000 a year from royalties." The unnamed record company is Arhoolie Records. Strachwitz also created multiple income lines from his involvement in the 1960 LP *Big Mama in Europe*, compensating himself as the author of its liner notes and the photographer for the cover.

The album was recorded at Wessex Sound Studios in Highbury New Park. The unique history of the studio speaks to a range of intersections that inspire me. Wessex Sound is where the Sex Pistols recorded *Never Mind the Bollocks* and the Clash recorded *London Calling*. It brings me deep satisfaction to know that Willie Mae was, indirectly, part of a punk narrative. At the core of her life as a wandering hustler is her relationship to DIY culture, which also situates punk as an anti-establishment (even when anti-Black) genre and movement. I found even more excitement in Willie Mae's recording experience at Wessex when I learned that Stevie Wonder, Prince, Björk, Queen, and David Bowie had recorded there as well.

Willie Mae's debut studio album makes me think about how she pronounced Europe in one and a half syllables, like "Eh-rope." It reminds me of how she'd drop the *g* off certain words (travelin') and replace an *i* with an *a* (sangin'). As Geneva Smitherman tells us in her explanation of Black English, Willie Mae made a new language with an old tongue. On *Big Mama in Europe*, she not only sings with complete confidence in her command of language and voice but also plays her instruments of choice — harmonica and drums.

Session players for the record were drawn from the American Folk Blues Festival crew, including Buddy Guy on guitar, Fred Below on drums, Eddie Boyd on piano and organ, and Jimmie Lee Robinson on bass. Both Walter "Shaky" Horton and Willie Mae played harmonica on a selection of tracks. Allmusic.com cites Willie Mae as a drummer on the songs "Your Love Is Where It Ought to Be" and "Session Blues." At times it's clear that the album, in a way, is a live rehearsal. The players are learning as they go and leaning into the magic that surfaces when they fully connect.

The album opens with "Sweet Little Angel," which I discussed in an earlier chapter as a great blues classic. Willie Mae performs it on most of her albums and it appeared on nearly all her compilations. The second song, "The Place," is not a traditional blues; instead, it has the sound of a Jamaican one-drop or rocksteady sound, which gestures toward her diasporic relevance in Black music-making. It also demonstrates her range, in both talent and musical interests. She references a "hound dog" in "The Place," though it doesn't match the tone or the lyrics. Instead, she uses the opportunity to remind listeners, once again, who did it first and better. "Little Red Rooster" is the third song, another blues standard. In this version, Eddie Boyd's organ holds steady throughout like he's leading a Black church processional. The song speaks to the thin line between blues and gospel, and there's a ghostly presence of those who had their way with the song before she had hers. The piece uses zoomorphism to describe a wandering lover and is complete with cackles and howls to describe this hound dog–ish man.

There's a new version of "Hound Dog" on *Big Mama in Europe*. The harmonica is more pronounced in this take, and her voice is confident and convincing. Whenever she sings or records "Hound Dog" throughout the years, she asserts, musically, her claim to the fortune that the song earned others. In this version, she offers skilled defiance in the slight adjustments to the song's structure through ad-libs and vocal intonations. "Swing It on Home" and "Honky Tonk" are clear examples of her relationship to the Memphis sound. In "Swing It on Home," the opening lyrics are "I wish I was an apple / Hanging from a tree / Have all the sweet little men / Reaching out for me / . . . / They gonna marry you someday." I heard a frisky daughter of a minister (like Aretha!) and was left with an awareness of how the studio carries some of the possibilities of a pulpit. Playfully, as the song ends, she proposes the idea of marrying the men in her band. She calls each of their names while singing "Marry you someday, E. Boyd / Marry you someday, Buddy Guy / Marry you someday, Jimmie Lee / Marry you someday, Fred McDowell." At one point in the song, Willie Mae even calls Chris Strachwitz's name, telling him that she wants him to know "this record is going back down to Alabama in the field of the corn." The lyric indicates that while she's recording in London, the heart of the song is back home where the soil is funky. Both "Swing It on Home" and "Honky Tonk" make audibly clear the close relationship between blues and country music and bring to mind the musical work of Charley Pride and Ray Charles, who dabbled in country music as well. It's fair to say that such familiarity is linked to both the Kentucky bluegrass hold on the banjo and the black folk who plucked new genres on strings based on region.

The album plays with a range of tempos. "Your Love Is Where It Ought to Be," for instance, is a low-down jook joint sermon. She leads with the harmonica and holds the rhythm with her work as a drummer. Both instruments along with her voice are prominent and demanding. Willie Mae includes two other songs with a similar tempo, "My Heavy Load" and "School Boy," both of which feature Mississippi Fred McDowell on electric slide guitar. There is a history lesson in this duet. McDowell, an Arhoolie labelmate, is famously associated with playing hill country blues. Thornton's and McDowell's shared grief—and lyrics that lift the heavy load—translates into legible sorrow in these numbers.

In "Session Blues," Willie Mae calls Buddy Guy's name again. Her discography shows that Willie Mae called on him many times throughout the years. The "Session Blues" and "Down Home Blues" are jam sessions that illustrate the camaraderie between the two in the studio. The songs speak to the fact that the two had been touring Europe for weeks, fighting, fussing, and creating magic as part of the American Folk Blues Festival. "Good Time in London" speaks to Willie Mae as a daughter of the Black Atlantic. The lyrics are feisty and ambiguous in terms of whom she's talking to: "Come here, baby / Sit down on Big Mama's knee / I just wanna whisper in your ear darling / Let you know what is worrying me / Come here." Willie Mae gives the impression that she enjoys the UK streets and that between her studio and performance work she might be making acquaintances with "Sweet Little Angels" or "Little Red Roosters," take your pick.

The Willie Mae blues are a story about place. They traveled wherever she landed. When she left London and headed back to Los Angeles in October 1965, she did so with new life experiences and memories. Touring abroad allowed her to understand her work and the blues outside of an American context. Baldwin and I also had a similar understanding. It's what happens when the social context and conditions of your citizenship are shifted and your passport helps you escape (even if temporarily) the confines of American racism. James Baldwin, Willie Mae, and I found ourselves stretched by the reach of the blues and our relationships with the blues. The blues in some form made the three of us clearer about our respective roles—as performers, ambassadors, and witnesses. The reality is that Willie Mae's work in Europe is but one song in the catalog of traveling blueswomen. There is no doubt that her coming back to the United States shifted the musical landscape on the West Coast again. Upon her return she penned another song that changed the course of music history, and she met the perfect white girl, whom she allowed to help her do it.

YOUR BLUES AIN'T LIKE MINE

Rock and roll, like practically every form of popular music across the globe, is Black music and we are its heirs. We, too, claim the right of creative freedom and access to American and International airwaves, audiences, markets, resources, and compensations, irrespective of genre.

GREG TATE

Willie Mae Thornton was two years old when Victoria Spivey recorded a song that projected the story of Willie Mae's life. Spivey's "Your Worries Ain't Like Mine" speaks to the early death of her protagonist's parents; she is left without people to "teach her right from wrong" and gets so drunk that she "lost her head." Spivey moans into the mic with a declaration that rings true for the experiences of Willie Mae Thornton and the blueswomen before her: "I'm five and worried / 'Cause no one cares for me." Blueswomen who found mothers on the road. Seventeen years after Willie Mae's birth, a white woman named Janis Lyn Joplin was born into a different hue of the blues. Her vocal depth arose from an ever-present pain, lyricized by Willie Mae Thornton in 1961 for a song called "Ball 'n' Chain."

Upon returning from her travel abroad, where she

helped spread the blues in Europe, Willie Mae continued to make her way up and down the California coast for most of the late 1960s. Janis Joplin and Willie Mae crossed paths at the Both/And club in San Francisco in 1966. The meeting brought welcome but unexpected changes to their respective lives. Joplin had long been a fan of Willie Mae Thornton and seeing her perform live was a big step in Joplin's artistic development. In her biography *Scars of Sweet Paradise: The Life and Times of Janis Joplin* Alice Echols quotes her praising Willie Mae in no uncertain terms: "She sings the blues with such heart and soul. I have learned so much from her and only wish I could sing as well as Willie Mae." The rest is history.

When Janis Joplin first started listening to the blues in Port Arthur, Texas, she was coming of age and leaning, even if clumsily, into her power. As a teenager, she dreamed of ditching her overbearing parents and mean-spirited classmates and distancing herself from the unique brand of Texas racism. One aspect of her rebellion was daring to interact with Black people through their music. Unlike the people who surrounded her, she thought of Black people as humans deserving of equality. Her early connection to the blues was a healthy distraction from regular bouts with bullying and a way to develop her role in the counterculture. Part of the aggression aimed at Janis was her refusal to perpetuate gender roles that threatened her freedom. She wore trousers, refused to wear makeup, and resisted many other trappings of femininity. To make matters worse, she struggled with weight-related issues and excessive acne. Janis Joplin found sanctuary in Black modes of expression. She appreciated the sounds Black people made and was empathetic to the experiences they storied through song.

The night Willie Mae and Janis met, Joplin, along with Big Brother and the Holding Company guitarist James Gurley, asked for permission to remake "Ball 'n' Chain." Spörke claims that Willie Mae was honored by the request. She handwrote the song's lyrics on a small piece of paper backstage and told them to "take it and sing it." Their version of "Ball 'n' Chain" upended the dubious practice of white artists covering Black music. To avoid simply copying the music of Black blues people, Big Brother rearranged the song and changed the key and tempo. Spörke and Echols explain how the group named this process "Big Brotherizing," which helped them push their voices as creators. Big Brother and the Holding Company premiered the song at the Monterey Pop Festival in 1967 and included a live version of "Ball 'n' Chain," recorded at the Filmore East, on their 1968 *Cheap Thrills* album. Willie Mae's response upon hearing Joplin's vocals was simple: "That girl feels like I do." In an interview published on April 6, 1970, Willie Mae told Ralph Gleason of the *San Francisco Chronicle* that "you got to really understand the blues to play the blues."

By the mid-1960s, Willie Mae was seen as a legend. Jimmy Moore, her manager at the time, helped her land and coordinate a range of high-profile gigs, including her first appearance at the Monterey Jazz Festival in 1964. Prestige from her association with the American Folk Blues Festival gave her the leverage she needed to negotiate performance fees when she returned to the States in 1965. Upon her return, Moore drew up and signed the release in 1966 for Big Brother and the Holding Company to perform "Ball 'n' Chain." The contract was signed even though publishing rights to Willie Mae's song were controlled by

Bay-Tone Records, where she first recorded it in 1961. The release of "Ball 'n' Chain" prompted legal battles. Spörke points out how Joplin's respect for Willie Mae resulted in a creative scheme to correctly credit her and get her paid for the song. Speaking to a reporter in 1972, Willie Mae was clear about the benefits she received because of Big Brother's offering: "I gave her the right and the permission to make 'Ball 'n' Chain.' . . . It's all right, it made me money. At least I got paid for it, and I'm still drawing royalties."

Willie Mae continued recording singles for small independent labels. In April 1966, she cut "Because It's Love" and "Life Goes On," two songs now part of a Bay Area pantheon of blues classics released by Galaxy Records. "Because It's Love" features Willie Mae on the harmonica, but her vocals do most of the work. "Life Goes On" is a slow blues that she returned to again and again on future albums and regularly performed at blues festivals across the United States.

Chris Strachwitz and his Arhoolie Records crew were the main organizers of many of those events. As a record producer, Strachwitz paired Willie Mae with blues musicians who matched her weight as an artist. Through his role as co-organizer of the Berkeley Blues Festival in 1966, he asked one of its performers, Muddy Waters, if he'd be interested in backing Willie Mae for her next album. Waters agreed, knowing there would be little to no time for rehearsal. *Big Mama Thornton with the Muddy Waters Blues Band* was released in 1966 as her second full album. As on her debut record, the magic came in the improvisational nature of the music and the connective tissue (the back home feeling) that bonded the group. Her sophomore album emerged from each musician's mastery, familiarity, trust, and faith. It's also a public record that speaks to the chemistry and lasting friendship between Waters and Thornton.

It sounds like a fusion of Southwest and West Coast blues as interpreted through a Chicago electric blues school. It's a poly-regional journey through songs like "I'm Feeling Alright," the up-tempo opening track, and "Gimmie a Penny," a slow blues funk that closes the album. Other songs, like "Black Rat" and "Wrapped Tight," are danceable blues jams inflected with Willie Mae's shouts and ad-libs. "Big Mama's Shuffle" is an instrumental that features Willie Mae and James Cotton calling and responding with the harmonica. Most of the album showcases downtempo traditional blues that roots each sound in place, a rendering of the "blues geography," as Clyde Woods called it, that speaks to the blues as a class-based cultural product of migration.

Big Mama with the Muddy Waters Band solidified her popularity as she actively performed between 1966 and 1969. Spörke points out that "Thornton was more and more in demand on campuses, in clubs, folk festivals, and rock festivals and would, with great success, play some of the biggest festivals, record new singles and albums and become a regular on the nightclub circuit." She and her manager used her fame and visibility to secure a second appearance at the Monterey Jazz Festival in 1966. Willie Mae was part of a Saturday afternoon program titled "Nothing but the Blues," and unsurprisingly she left the audience hungry for more. Fans of multiple genres responded favorably to Willie Mae's artistry. She was a hit on the blues scene, the R&B scene, the folk scene, the festival circuit, the jazz scene, and the highbrow crowd at New

York's Museum of Modern Art. The range in venues she played shows just how compelling she was as a performer.

Willie Mae's zigzag movement between a residency at the Ash Grove in Los Angeles and performances at the Filmore West in San Francisco with rock groups like Jefferson Airplane and the Grateful Dead in the Bay Area expanded her reach. She held another residency at the Jazz Workshop in San Francisco and participated in jam sessions with jazz musicians like the Joe Henderson Quartet and Elvin Jones. She belonged everywhere, including Carnegie Hall. In 1967 Willie Mae performed there with the Count Basie Orchestra as part of John Hammond's thirtieth anniversary *From Spirituals to Swing* show. Hammond, a white, liberal producer and talent scout, was one of the most influential individuals in twentieth century American popular music. He "discovered" Billie Holiday and is credited with launching the careers of such prominent artists as Bob Dylan and Aretha Franklin.

I learned about Hammond's legacy through a song written and performed by Prince titled "Avalanche" from his *One Nite Alone . . .* album (2002). Lyrically, Prince spares none of the men he exposes as faux friends of Black Americans over centuries. The song opens with a verse critiquing Abraham Lincoln and the myth of his role as the Great Emancipator. The verse that follows turns to Hammond: "Who's that lurking in the shadows? / Mr. John Hammond with his pen in hand / Sayin' sign your kingdom over to me / And be known throughout the land." Prince isn't buying Hammonds's good intentions — "like every snowflake in the avalanche" — and his take is consistent with his decades-long battle with music executives and the labels they represent.

Tarnishing Hammond's legacy is part of the activist work Prince did to call attention to the unfair treatment of Black artists. Willie Mae was part of that legacy. However, while John Hammond's *From Spirituals to Swing* show was a significant opportunity for her, I can't help but wonder how Willie Mae and the other artists were compensated. Though the exposure generated opportunities for the performers, they certainly were not paid as much as the white show producers were.

Black blueswomen could not escape the perils of racialized and gendered business practices. Willie Mae's career points to how critics of the music industry's neo-plantation dynamic should be considered advocates for social justice. Black music activists. That said, we have to reckon with the Black managers who exploited Willie Mae throughout her career as well. After three years with Jimmy Moore, Willie Mae was approached by another character offering managerial support. His name was Archie Moore, a former boxer who had little experience in the music industry. Inexplicably, according to both her biographer and observations by Jimmy Moore, she entered into this professional relationship quite recklessly despite others warning her of professional danger. Staying with the plantation metaphor, Archie (and Don Robey and Suge Knight and Berry Gordy) could be seen as overseers, pawns in the plantation ecosystem, scheming their way to more capital at the expense of their people.

It was 1967 when Willie Mae decided to change managers from Jimmy Moore to Archie Moore. She made this move while still in high demand as a performer. In response, Jimmy Moore sued her for breach of contract. He won the suit and never worked with her again. In his absence, her gigs grew less prestigious. She began playing the small club circuit again. Before the end of the year, Willie Mae hit a wall with Archie Moore and severed ties with him too. During the interim, she sought Bob Messinger, Muddy Waters's manager, and continued to perform multiple times a week throughout 1967 to promote *Big Mama Thornton with the Muddy Waters Blues Band*. Once again she was culturally popular and professionally vulnerable, and her motivation for the choice in managers is unclear. Ultimately, it was her decision.

In 1968 Willie Mae returned to Harlem's Apollo Theater and shared the stage with Odetta, T-Bone Walker, Big Joe Turner, and others. She also returned to the Monterey Jazz Festival for the final time. Arhoolie, riding the wave of excitement around her work, released what would be her last album on the label, *Ball 'n' Chain*, with almost the same set of songs from her first album, *Big Mama in Europe*. Strachwitz saw an opportunity to capitalize on the success of the "Ball 'n' Chain" cover by Big Brother and Holding Company. The album was recorded at the Coast Recorders in San Francisco. Willie Mae's "Ball 'n' Chain," much like "Hound Dog," generated a wave of profits for various music executives and other artists.

Janis Joplin's relationship with Willie Mae Thornton's "Ball 'n' Chain" gave me a new way to think about the precarity of white women's sonic lives. I understand Willie Mae's affection for Joplin and why she paused almost every time she performed the song and spoke Janis Joplin's name. "Ball 'n' Chain" represents a kind of post-Elvis emotional justice for Willie Mae Thornton. Big Brother's cover allowed Willie Mae to gain some of the material resources and acclaim owed to her, though it came twenty years into her career. While there is no doubt that Janis Joplin benefited from an industry that awarded white women who performed Black music, she is a valuable case study because she complicates the notion of appropriation.

Maureen Mahon writes extensively about white women who participated in the disappearance of Black women musicians, specifically those Black women who served as models for the most celebrated white rockers across gender. In her discussion of cover songs, she names women who resisted the whitewashing of Black music. *Black Diamond Queens* tells us the many ways LaVern Baker wasn't having it. She raised hell and spoke publicly about racist industry practices. To highlight Baker's resistance, Mahon shared the example of how, "just two weeks after Baker's version of 'Tweedlee Dee' appeared on the pop charts, [Georgia] Gibbs's version, released on Mercury Records, followed. Gibbs's record outsold Baker's and reached number two on the pop charts. . . . But Baker was outspoken in her condemnations of covers. . . . What she took issue with was the appropriation of the part of the song that was hers: the arrangement." Mahon also highlights Ruth Brown in her exploration of race, gender, and covers: "Many R&B artists suffered from the cover crisis that Baker decried. Mercury's Patti Page hit the *Billboard* Top 40 copying Ruth Brown's 'Oh, What a Dream,' while Brown's version only made it to the R&B charts; to add insult to injury, Page's version crossed over the R&B charts." It's in Baker's arrangement argument that you'll find the ghost of "Hound Dog," since Willie Mae arranged her own vocals on the tune.

Five years after Aretha Franklin became the first woman to be inducted into the Rock and Roll Hall of Fame, LaVern

Baker followed in 1991. While considered the industry's highest honor, it's hard to see Rock Hall induction as anything but a symbolic, white boy magic gatekeeping institution that fancies itself the all-knowing judge of cultural relevance. An institution that wields its power, influence, and resources to determine who should be honored and remembered (and who shouldn't). More snowflakes in the avalanche. It's important to point out that Janis Joplin was inducted into the Rock and Roll Hall of Fame (the same year as Ruth Brown, in 1993), but Willie Mae has yet to be honored — not even as an Early Influence Award recipient, which she undoubtedly earned and deserves. I have no shame in repeating this fact and calling out the hypocrisy again and again. I also want to believe that Joplin would have refused to accept the honor, knowing Willie Mae had been snubbed for decades. That's what Teena Marie would have done.

There are differences between white women like Janis Joplin and Teena Marie, but both have earned respect from generations of Black women. One thing that separates Joplin and Marie from Georgia Gibbs and Patti Page is that they moved through their entire careers citing Black people, Black music, and specifically Black women as their primary sources of inspiration. This showed up in interviews, on stage, and for Teena Marie, in the music itself. She called attention to race and Black music, artists, writers, and even cuisine, shaping her rhythmic calling and musical purpose. In the song "Square Biz," she spoke directly to Black listeners: "I've been called Casper, Shorty, Lil' Bit / And some they call me Vanilla Child / But you know that don't mean my world to me / 'Cause baby, names can't cramp my style." Later in the verse, she lists her influences and pays homage: "You know I love spirituals and rock / Sarah Vaughan, Johann Sebastian Bach / Shakespeare, Maya Angelou / And Nikki Giovanni just to name a few." Teena Marie made her position known for the permanent record, and "Square Biz" might be one of the most widely heard and memorized songs in Black social dance spaces since its release in 1980.

Janis Joplin listened to and learned from Willie Mae. Allured by Thornton's audible authenticity, she found herself identifying with the hardships Willie Mae encountered as a target of racism and sexism and as a champion of artful shouting. She was also impressed by Billie Holiday and Aretha Franklin. The 2015 documentary *Janis Joplin: Little Girl Blue* included footage of Janis describing what she gained from close listening to the two: "They are so subtle, they could milk you with two notes. They could go no further than from A to B, and they can make you feel like they told you the whole universe. . . . I don't know that yet, all I got now is strength, but maybe if I keep singing, I'll get it." Throughout her career, Joplin described the unique impact that Willie Mae had on her as an artist, but she also spoke to her intimate relationship with blues people across the board. Learning from Memphis Minnie to Leadbelly, and hundreds of artists in between, Janis Joplin understood that the true blues revival was in understanding the transformative nature of the blues on its creators and listeners. She understood the blues as a healing force and appreciated Willie Mae Thornton as a critical voice who used this power. Maybe that's why Nina Simone understood Janis Joplin too.

I was never quite sure why at the 1976 Montreux Jazz Festival Nina Simone shared that she had seen the Janis

Joplin film. She didn't mention the title, but she's referring to the 1974 documentary film titled *Janis*. Nina told the crowd that she started to write a song about it, "but I decided you weren't worthy." She was speaking to the predominantly white audience, who she felt were there just for the festival. The implication was that they did not want to hear about the inner life of Nina Simone, the circumstances and experiences that brought her hands to the keys and her music to the stage. "It pained me to see how hard [Janis Joplin] worked because she got hooked into a thing, it wasn't on drugs, she got hooked into a feeling, and she played to corpses." She then tsk-tsked the crowd, scorning them for being among the dead. She spoke with a microphone in her right hand while wearing a black dress and sporting a short afro and toned arms. She laughed as she carefully stepped over the mic cord and strutted across the stage. Simone was mocking the audience in Janis's honor. Janis's biography captures her being equally vocal about giving to but not receiving enough from audiences. It's amazing that Nina folded all these layers into her set list.

Joplin also was the inspiration for the 1974 song "Nightbird," written by Nona Hendryx, which appears on Labelle's *Nightbirds* album. A key moment happens when Patti Labelle composes a vocal eulogy with a highly specialized run stretching out the lyrics "She feeds the fire of a flame" as if trying to capture Joplin's entire lifetime. The song is full of heartbreak and celebration of a woman whom they saw as suffering because "Nightbird's sky is never high enough / She only touches down / Just to fill her wings again."

The incredible display of public affection for Janis Joplin from Black women tells us a story about the blues as a kind of "woman's work" that can break open new dimensions of connectedness through artistically rich sadness. Joplin bought a headstone for the grave of Bessie Smith, who had been lying in an unmarked grave. Memphis Minnie, also buried in an unmarked grave, was given her due props when Bonnie Raitt led the effort to place a granite headstone at her resting place one hundred years after her death. Alice Walker and Charlotte Hunt found the unmarked the grave of Zora Neale Hurston in 1973 as part of a ceremonial excavation project and made sure a new headstone would ensure she'd be remembered. These women — Janis, Bonnie, Alice, and Charlotte — found a way to mother the spirits of the dead and challenge antiquated views about race in the process. But *America Eats Its Young*, as the Funkadelic album says, and race still rears its ugly head.

After an entire century of Black women creating the blueprint for the blues, British rock, and American rock 'n' roll, the rock industry referred to Janis as "Queen of the Blues," which is not only ludicrous but a title I assume she would reject. However, Joplin referred to herself as a "white Black woman," a move that was equally curious and jarring. Such a statement could be injurious to the mental health of some Black women who suffer the material consequences of misogynoir, as Moya Bailey calls it. In 1992, Bebe Moore Campbell published *Your Blues Ain't Like Mine*, a novel about racialized violence in Mississippi and the psychological repercussions that extend from generation to generation. The title of her book, which I'm assuming was inspired by Victoria Spivey's song, is a fitting response to Joplin. There are no white kings and queens of the blues, but there are white shouters. Janis is one of them, and you can hear this in the emotional crescendo of "Ball 'n' Chain."

Those who know the song intimately wait for this peak, and Willie Mae always took it very seriously. It arrives after the third verse, and though Willie Mae typically changes the lyrics, the crescendo is still there for the taking. It's a return to the chorus where she sings, "I said oh, oh Baby / Why do you wanna do all these mean things to me?" But she shouts it, making it clear that the "Ball 'n' Chain" and the weight of this love are heavy enough to hold her back. She lets it all out. And so does Janis when she steps up to the peak that Willie Mae designed. It is here that I hear the intersections of their lives, the shared but distinct struggles that made it possible for Willie Mae to write the song and for Janis to earn the right to sing it.

Janis Joplin's ashes were scattered in the Pacific Ocean, which makes perfect sense. She represents a rare tidal wave of emotion whose musical life was extended by Willie Mae's complex music creation. Willie Mae's courage and fierce commitment to her artistry gave Janis her wings. So now, who will find the unmarked grave of Willie Mae and allow her to rest?

MIXTAPES, WHITE BIOGRAPHERS, AND BLACK BLUES PEOPLE

America, so frequently, is excited about the stories of black people but not the black people themselves.

HANIF ABDURRAQIB

The intimate relationship I have with Willie Mae exists in part because of the biography written by Michael Spörke. Her story so compelled me — the way he told it, the research he did, and the care he displayed — that I traveled to Düsseldorf to meet him. I contacted Spörke immediately following my discovery of his book. His response was generous enough that I asked if he'd be willing to speak to me in person. Taken aback by my willingness to cross oceans, he agreed, and we settled on a date. Before reaching out, I searched for pictures of Spörke on the internet. He was a white German man with kind eyes. My reading of him was significant, considering that I would be making the journey to meet him alone. A range of dark things could have occurred, but I took the chance. This was for Willie Mae, and I felt an added level of protection with that.

I flew from Los Angeles to Berlin and took the train to

Düsseldorf. The passengers' faces were serious and stoic, heavy with a history of violence etched into their skin. I thought about concentration camps and the German colonies in Africa. Despite their history of violence, Germans led the so-called blues revival in Europe, and it was German men—from Willie Mae's biographer Michael Spörke, to her producer at Arhoolie Records Chris Strachwitz, to Horst Lippmann and Fritz Rau, the men who organized the American Folk Blues Festival—who took the most interest in her career. And now, here I was interacting with one of those German men. I must admit that Spörke, with the same spirit of care he offered Willie Mae, arranged for me to be picked up from the train station. When I called to inform him of my arrival, he mentioned, very casually, that we'd both be easy to find because I was Black and he was in a wheelchair—implying that we'd be two rarities at the station. Until that point, I assumed he was a cishet, able-bodied white man with access to all the privileges such an identity affords.

Düsseldorf was foreign to me. I started my journey with Willie Mae from a distant place. I felt distant from the city and Michael Spörke. What, then, does this distance mean for Willie Mae's story? How had her life found a home in the space between Spörke's and mine? Had Willie Mae arranged this? Because yes, there was distance but also undeniable connections between Spörke and me. For one, our respective places on the margins of society make our telling her story an unlikely tag-teaming that she perhaps orchestrated. If you believe in ghosts as I do.

Once we arrived at Spörke's house, I set up my camera and placed a lapel mic on his collar. We then entered the world of Willie Mae. He explained how he had learned of her from research he conducted for his biography on Big Brother and the Holding Company. "I heard about Big Mama through 'Ball 'n' Chain,' and one thing that stood out to me is that Big Brother, Janis Joplin in particular, always mentioned her name before performing her song." I shared that I, too, discovered Willie Mae upon stumbling on a live performance of "Ball 'n' Chain" on a television show called *Mixed Bag* on WGBH in 1970. When I asked Spörke why he decided to write a book about Willie Mae's life, he shared that he was "only interested in musicians and biographies that no one has written, because it's boring to write about people who've already been written about."

Spörke also told me that he began writing Willie Mae's biography with a goal in mind: to highlight her musicianship and dispel the myth that she was an aggressive lesbian known for her struggle with alcohol. "I tried to find out more about Big Mama. There was little information about the music, just sensational things. The members of Big Brother Holding Company spoke differently about her." He felt one of his greatest challenges was the waning access he had to the now-elderly witnesses of Willie Mae's career, "It was nice to talk to all the musicians and get the stories firsthand. So, I looked for musicians who played with her. Many people gave me the names of other musicians and contact numbers, which was the process. By the end of it, I had spoken to over one hundred people for the book. Many of those musicians were beginning to die a year later, including Big Walter Price from Houston. When we first spoke, he was nearly one hundred. He died very soon after our interview."

Spörke's biography was vital to my work, but I was honest with him about my annoyance that he was white. In response, he shook his head vigorously in agreement, following up with "Sure, of course." He then reflected on his position as a white biographer:

> I knew what it looked like going in, me a white man writing about Big Mama, but I'm interested in music. I entered Black music through Janis Joplin. I was fourteen years old when I heard her for the first time. If you are a lover of blues and you listen to white blues artists, the next step has to be to go to the originals, so I did that, I went to Muddy Waters and Buddy Guy. Once I discovered the originals, I realized that the white artists were just a copy. They were not the originals. For Willie Mae, I went from "Ball 'n' Chain" to "Hound Dog," and when I heard her version of "Hound Dog," well, I forgot about Elvis.

"Hound Dog" was included on *Stronger Than Dirt* (1969), an album she recorded upon leaving Arhoolie and signing with Mercury Records. Although she included the song on most of her albums, she often changed its structure to solidify her ownership. On this record she introduces a dance-floor jazz version. "Ball 'n' Chain" appears on *Stronger Than Dirt* as well, only this time she slows it down to an unrecognizable blues number radically different from Big Brother's cover. It could be argued that this version is, too, a reclamation, an insistence that no one but Willie Mae *knows* these songs — her respect for Janis notwithstanding. *Stronger Than Dirt* also includes "Summertime," casting Willie Mae among the hundreds of artists who covered George Gershwin's classic, including Joplin. Admittedly, Joplin's version moves me more than Willie Mae's.

Still, Willie Mae shows her range and includes a prominent organ part, harking back to her Black church roots.

Other songs on the album hint at Willie Mae's recognition of the transformation the blues were undergoing with the involvement of white folk artists. Willie Mae covers Bob Dylan's "I Shall Be Released" and "That Lucky Song," written by American songwriting duo Beasley Smith and Haven Gillespie. While white cultural appropriation is a topic that raises eyebrows in the context of Black American music, one must acknowledge the intriguing performances of Black musicians who cover the work of white musicians. Bob Dylan, who was said to have had one of the biggest influences on Jimi Hendrix, has famously been covered by a considerable number of Black artists — enough to inspire the 2010 compilation *How Many Roads: Black America Sings Bob Dylan*. Nina Simone covered at least five Dylan songs throughout her career. Perhaps one of the key differences between white artists covering the songs originally written and performed by Black artists and Black artists covering songs originally written and performed by white musicians is the question of publishing rights and the ownership of masters. Given the racialized exploitation of Black artists within the music industry — especially when white artists cover songs written by Black musicians — Black performers (who might have been swindled through shady contracts or forced by producers to share publishing rights) might never see any money. Yet Willie Mae, one of those artists who lost the rights to many of the songs she wrote, covered Bob Dylan.

Another exciting element of the *Stronger Than Dirt* album is her stunning performance of up-tempo soulful songs like "Let's Go Get Stoned," written by Ashford and Simpson, and "Funky Broadway," written by Arlester "Dyke" Christian of Dyke and the Blazers in 1966 and credited as one of the first songs to use the word "funk" in its title. The latter is about a dance and gives instructions on how "to do the Funky Broadway." Consistent with her covers, however, Willie Mae repurposes the lyrics and reconstructs the song's theme. Her version describes going into a club and discovering the song "Funky Broadway" on the jookbox. The club scene is interrupted when "A big police walked in / He said looka hear you people make too much noise / I'll just have to run you in / So he took us all to jail / Didn't no one come and pay my bail / So I went there and had to face that judge / I said judge, your honor, I'm not guilty / What he told you was a lie / . . . / I said judge it sho was funky." There are no references to police officers, jail, or judges in the original song or any other covers (by Wilson Pickett, the Supremes, the Temptations, Jimmy Smith, and many others). This is one of the most fantastic examples of her legacy as a blues emcee, demonstrating the blues impulse that roots itself in Willie Mae's innovative lyrical and freestyle skills.

Her cover of "Funky Broadway" shows that Willie Mae didn't surrender to the demand that the market placed on blues artists to embrace a rock-oriented album. She doubled down on that refusal with her second Mercury studio album, *The Way It Is* (1970). Throughout the album she stays grounded in the soul, R&B, gospel, and blues that defined her sound, passion, and career. Her commitment to working-class Black music stood against the commercial success to be had by appealing to the rock crowd. *The Way It Is* is made up of Willie Mae standards like "Little Red Rooster," "One Black Rat," and "Sweet Little Angel."

"Baby Please Don't Go / Got My Mojo Workin'" sounds like funkified Black church blues. Her voice is skillfully raspy, quiet when it needs to be and explosive when the lyrics call for it, such as when she addresses the changing political climate by singing "We have a new governor out here in California called Ronald Reagan / He don' cut off my welfare check / I'd like to know what he gonna cut off next."

"Don't Need No Doctor" features Willie Mae singing about failing health when, indeed, her health was poor. Though there is no evidence that she performed this song to reflect her personal life, managers and fellow artists did tell her to slow down, noticing her thinning body. Despite their advice, her drinking continued. The blues provided Willie Mae opportunities to play with the truth. Equally powerful was her relationship to old Negro spirituals. Willie Mae takes the well-known spiritual "Wade in the Water" and sneaks in a few references to "Hound Dog." In our Düsseldorf interview, Spörke pointed to her resilience and artistic integrity, pausing at the fact that her career started in the 1940s and ended in the 1980s. He emphasized that she never stopped performing or recording: "If you listen to her last records, when she was already very sick, her voice was still the same, powerful till the end. . . . It wasn't so easy for musicians, but you can still hear that music was her life."

It's fair to say that my musical education started with memorizing full albums and reading music biographies. As a result, I've had to reckon with biographies and memoirs of Black folk as a contested site. Biographies, though positioned as an objective genre of literature, are part of a history of racialized (and gendered) exclusions from

publishing houses, academic institutions, and rock jour-
nals, which act as gatekeepers determining which music
deserves to be remembered. In *Whose Blues? Facing Up to
Race and the Future of the Music*, Adam Gussow points to a
pattern that surfaced in the 1990s when there was a "flow-
ering of black blues autobiographies by Sammy Price,
Mance Lipscomb, Willie Dixon, B. B. King, David Hon-
eyboy Edwards, Ruth Brown, Yank Rachell, and Henry
Townsend; the next decade and a half added the life stories of Etta James and Buddy Guy." In every case, he says,
"black vernacular voices were shaped into print by white
ghostwriters."

The white author/Black blues dynamic continued
into the 2010s when several white and non-Black women
wrote biographies on Nina Simone, Sarah Vaughan, Memphis Minnie, Bessie Smith, Ma Rainey, and Sister Rosetta
Tharpe. In particular, the biography of Sister Rosetta
Tharpe written by Gayle Wald had a monumental impact
on recuperating her legacy and setting the stage for Tharpe
to be recognized for her musicianship and inducted into
the Rock and Roll Hall of Fame in 2018. The concern is
less about the fact that the biographies were written by
non-Black people and more about the inequity that makes
writing about Black musical lives violently inaccessible to
Black writers and thinkers.

Adam Gussow also drew my attention to a 1969 Muddy
Waters album titled *Fathers and Sons* and to the commentary offered by the Black Arts Movement writer Ron Welburn that Gussow cites in his book. Welburn identifies the
album as "rock's attempt to imitate the city blues of the
forties and fifties." He also claims that white guitarist Paul
Butterfield, who plays on the record, worshiped Muddy
Waters, and he describes how that worship led to "a black

fathers / white sons syndrome." The cover of the album features a Black God giving the life-touch, à la Michelangelo's *Creation of Adam*, to a white neo-Greek hippie in shades. "This is part of the Euro-American scheme," Welburn says. "The black music impetus is only to be recognized as sire to the white world; a kind of wooden-Indian or buffalo-nickel wish. A vampirish situation indeed!"

Father and Sons was a collaboration between Waters and a new generation of white blues artists. The "fathers" were the Black blues legends Muddy Waters, Buddy Miles, Sam Lay, and Otis Spann, and the sons, born a generation or two later, were the white musicians Michael Bloomfield and Paul Butterfield. The songs were a combination of live performances and studio sessions. The album was strategically marketable (to white audiences) because it brought together Chicago urban blues and rock 'n' roll for the purpose of making a case for continuity and the fluidity of genre. Gussow shares that the father and son gimmick was a response to the purported decline in Black interest in the blues, coupled with white bluesmen who, not as sons but as resourced paternal figures, believed they valued the music more than its Black creators did. To be clear, white patrons' interest in saving the blues did not necessarily extend to improving the social conditions to which the blues responded.

Three years after *Father and Sons* was released, Willie Mae Thornton performed at the University of Oregon, in Eugene, on October 20, 1971, backed by the majority-white Paul Butterfield Blues Band. It was filmed by a crew from the television series *Gunsmoke* and became a documentary directed by Toby Byron titled *Gunsmoke Blues*. The film featured several musicians from the *Fathers and Sons* album: Muddy Waters, Paul Butterfield, Joe Turner,

George "Harmonica" Smith, Bee Houston, and J. B. Hutto. Willie Mae Thornton played a prominent role in the documentary as well.

It is impossible to say for sure, but I believe that Willie Mae's performance at the Oregon show speaks to the isolation one can feel when the musicians and the audience are mostly white and financial vulnerability necessitates one's involvement. Pondering this isolation, I recalled something Michael Spörke pointed to when talking about his decision to write a book about Willie Mae: "When I started the research, I always read that she was a dangerous and wild person that punched people, that she was a lesbian alcoholic with a knife and a pistol, that she made fun of musicians on the stage." As much as I appreciate his desire to clear her name, there are performances that indeed involve a drunk and belligerent Willie Mae making fun of her (white) musicians on stage. Spörke, in his biography, includes testimonies from a number of musicians who spoke about being humiliated by Willie Mae. However, my interpretation of her behavior was that Willie Mae was protective of the blues and called out the white musicians' lack of connection to the music itself or the life experiences that produced it. I state with confidence that Willie Mae was a blues purist and, as some would argue, a blues scholar.

Willie Mae's performance begins when she walks through the majority-white crowd, making her way to the stage. She weaves between reaching hands while playing the harmonica. In her opening song, Willie Mae blows more than she sings; in a high-energy rendition of "Early in the Morning," she blends in a version of Sam Cooke's "Chain Gang," a familiar interlude during her live shows.

At times she seems to be doing more on the harmonica than what the combined four members of the band are doing with their instruments. In between blowing harmonica, she sings with two mics in one hand. The camera pans the white crowd, and many of them don't seem to know how to move with the music. The odd tension on stage mirrors their collective awkward sway. When the camera zooms out to show Willie Mae's whole body, she's wearing a low afro with no earrings. Her accessories include an ascot scarf and a bolo tie. She's also sporting a cream-colored, smock-like blouse in the shape of a printless dashiki and matching pants. Dressed like the political discourse of the time — a Black nationalist Texan — she's a veteran artist leading the constantly-catching-up, mostly white band.

It's clear that if Willie Mae were white, the music would be called rock 'n' roll, which is to say that it's both her Blackness and her "female masculinity" (as Halberstam calls it) that makes the music legible as blues and illegible as rock 'n' roll. When the camera lands on her face, the spaces between her teeth come alive — gaps that operate like tunnels. When she wails and shouts, she produces sounds that shoot out from multiple directions in her mouth. Toward the end of "Ball 'n' Chain," she tries to nudge the band into some kind of crescendo, expecting them to hit the rhythm on the one. They missed the opportunity and Willie Mae, seasoned as she was, simply plays it off. If missing the cue wasn't enough, the guitarist, at one point, stands there resting both hands on his instrument. But Willie Mae comes from a more communal style of playing where chasing the rhythm through the unpredictable movement of the director keeps you on your toes, ready to fall in line or be penalized for missing the beat. Still, her performance was electrifying. Willie Mae tries her best to lead them to Black sonic connectivity, but the struggle remains visible and audible throughout the show. Nevertheless, the live performance did precisely what the album *Fathers and Sons* set out to do, ushering in a younger generation of white fans who were excited to see the Black origins of rock music.

Toward the end of the performance, Willie Mae welcomes everyone (Muddy, Big Joe Turner, George the Harmonica, etc.) back to the stage, and now she's wearing a cowboy hat. There's a slight slur as she introduces the lineup, but she's clear and proud of how she holds her liquor. When the Black musicians return to the stage, Willie Mae is back home again, even when faced with the majority-white Eugene crowd. If I listen carefully, I can hear Willie Mae in the back of my head saying, "I knew they weren't feeling the music and didn't understand it, but Big Mama gotta eat." This kind of trade-off complicates the role that racialized and gendered capitalism played in the so-called decline of the blues and the power structures that keep artists indebted to white interests.

A fascinating line of questions surfaced following this performance and Willie Mae's history as a blues musician in general. First, why was Willie Mae the only woman on the *Gunsmoke Blues* tour? Did the constant pairing with bluesmen distort where she fit in the genealogy of blueswomen? How does Willie Mae Thornton work in a conversation about *Fathers and Sons* of the blues? And finally, what gets lost in the translation when white biographers find themselves less inclined or less able to root the story of Black music in the history of white American violence? We need more biographical mixtapes on blueswomen by Black queer DJs to get the answers.

SAVED BY THE *AMAZING GRACE* OF MAHALIA JACKSON

I don't worry too much about the script, I just ad-lib, like Pearl Bailey.

MAHALIA JACKSON

I can't read music but I know where I'm singing.

WILLIE MAE THORNTON

You could call my piano my trademark, or one of my trademarks.

ARETHA FRANKLIN

Like Al Green, Marvin Gaye, and Nina Simone, Willie Mae Thornton, the child of a preacher, couldn't resist the pull of spiritual funk. She spent the early seventies joining forces on opposite ends of the spectrum of Black American music: god's music and the devil's music. Singing from the place she described to Studs Terkel in 1970 as being "in between all of it," Willie Mae signed with Pentagram Records in 1971 and recorded *Saved*, her long-imagined gospel album. The album is a culmination and living document of thirty years of mixing the elements of church music with the blues. In her interview with Strachwitz, she shared, "I would like very much to do spirituals because I feel like I got the voice, I feel like I got the power. I just feel like I can just do them." Connecting that confidence to her daily listening practice, she added, "You'd be surprised, mostly my occupation every morning is to turn on my radio and listen to spirituals." She shared a roster of gospel legends who inspired her most, like "the Dixie Hummingbirds, the Soul Stirrers, Mahalia Jackson, the Davis Sisters, the Five Blind Boys of Mississippi." The use of the word "occupation" stands out. It could refer to the job of listening to music as a fellow musician or the state of being occupied as in engaged. Both references speak to the professionalization of Willie Mae's ear and the spiritual-oriented sounds that helped her rise with each day.

Miles Davis once said, "Jazz is like the blues with a shot of heroin," which prompted me to sit more carefully with Willie Mae's movement through the jazz scene in the '70s. From Duke Ellington to Charles Mingus (who was in the audience when Willie Mae performed at the Museum of Modern Art gig in New York and whom she met after the show), she was recognized as a musical force by some of the premier jazz musicians. However, Willie Mae's statement on jazz reveals a person who was unimpressed by its hype. In a conversation with Michael Erlewine (quoted in Spörke's biography), one of the Ann Arbor Blues Festival organizers, where she performed in 1970, said, "Jazz? I don't understand it in the first place. It don't have no ending. Here he is up there blowin' and maybe he blow till he get tired, then he just stop." Her reflection (and the Black humor subtext it signaled) made me think about race, class, and music as interlocking categories that explain why jazz is associated with northern, literate, middle-class (bourgeois) players and listeners. Blues and R&B were more related to working-class politics. Willie Mae's alignment with the blues reinforced her social position as a working-poor southern woman steeped in Black oral traditions, not necessarily literary ones.

Miles Davis also said, with a measure of impatience, "We're not going to play the blues anymore, let the white folks play the blues, they got 'em so they can keep 'em." Willie Mae was more protective of the blues and she may not have understood jazz, but jazz understood Willie Mae. Her invitations to prestigious festivals (Newport, San Francisco Jazz Workshop, Jazz in the Garden, etc.) make that clear. Herbie Hancock's "Watermelon Man" is one of the few jazz tunes she covered and most certainly one of the only songs she fully lyricizes. I also know that jazz and R&B are born from elements of the blues. When you place Willie Mae at the intersection of gospel, soul, jazz, rock, funk, and blues—where she belongs—you'll also find Aretha Franklin and Mahalia Jackson.

There are history lessons found where the lives of Jackson, Franklin, and Thornton overlap. This link is especially present during the culturally defining years of 1970–72. In the early seventies, gospel music existed in close proximity to Black nationalism. Radical organizers would meet up in churches. Even the Black Arts Movement bares this close connection as demonstrated by Nikki Giovanni's poetry albums with the New York Community Choir. Aretha Franklin, a devout Baptist, wore a short afro and aligned herself with more militant movements, including her public support and offering of bail money to help free Angela Davis in 1970. Mahalia Jackson brought an end to her Christian-centered civil rights work with Ralph David Abernathy and Martin Luther King in the late '60s but kept her eyes and ears on the younger, more fiery activists like Diane Nash and Stokely Carmichael from SNCC. Stokely is credited with coining "Black Power" as an expression to organize voters in Mississippi. As a Californian throughout the '60s and early '70s, Willie Mae was never far from Oakland, where the Black Panther Party was founded. Her commentary about the LAPD appears in the introduction to "Little Red Rooster" on the 1970 *The Way It Is* album (recorded live in Los Angeles in 1968), which complemented the Panthers' fearless rhetoric aimed at the state. Willie Mae and the Panthers found a common enemy in California's carceral system and its right-wing governor, Ronald Reagan.

As Willie Mae conceptualized *Saved*, funk music emerged from a new articulation of Black working-class music — different from Motown's aspirational and integrationist-focused middle-class catalog. Berry Gordy uprooted his music-making factory and transplanted it to Los Angeles in 1972, where Motown shifted its focus to films like *Lady Sings the Blues* (1972) and *Mahogany* (1975). The Motown move followed a decision made by Al Bell, president of Stax Records, to travel from Memphis to Los Angeles to plan and produce the 1972 Wattstax concert.

Philly International Records was forging a regional sound on the East Coast with the wickedly talented producers Gamble and Huff in 1971. Curtis Mayfield's *Superfly* soundtrack, a brilliant mockery of the burgeoning Blaxploitation era (especially in his counter-lyrical critique of the film's themes), was released in 1972. And during this same era, James Brown was crowned the "Godfather of

Soul" and entered an official relationship with Polydor Records to create some of the 1970s' most crucial funk music. Brown's funk was source material for breakbeats and the DJ cultural practice of sampling that took shape in New York City less than a decade later. Some could argue that gospel was the catalyst for all these genre developments. The church was the first cultural institution for Black Americans—the place where field songs became pulpit hymns and jook joint jams. Gospel was a product of its environment as much as it shaped it.

Aretha, Mahalia, and Willie Mae were the daughters of Baptist minister fathers, and the daughters of mothers who died early. By 1971, Mahalia Jackson had spent twenty years as one of the most legendary voices in the golden age of the gospel movement. She worked, traveled, and built a unique expression of Black faith with longtime musical companion Thomas Dorsey, who began his career writing blues songs for Ma Rainey. Dorsey, a regular player on the Chicago blues scene, felt called by the Lord to turn his hands over to the music of the church. According to the Songwriters Hall of Fame website, Dorsey attended a Baptist convention and "was so moved by the musical preacher he heard that night that he had a conversion experience, coining the term, 'Gospel Music,' and writing his very first gospel song all within a week." He continued touring the blues circuit and developed gospel music at the same time. The union between Mahalia and Thomas is a seamless blend of gospel and the blues. It highlights the genres' interdependence. Mahalia also worked closely with Herbert Brewster, the Memphis minister whose East Trigg Baptist Church piqued Elvis Presley's curiosity. Presley spent much of the 1950s steeped in the sounds of

Black faith at East Trigg, and Brewster played a prominent role in shaping Presley's cadence and comfort with Black music. Mahalia also built a lifetime relationship with her pianist Mildred Falls, a dark-skinned, thick woman who soundtracked Mahalia's voice for over twenty years. We heard Mildred just as much as we heard Mahalia; she was an equal force, even if rarely seen.

Mahalia Jackson was from New Orleans, a descendent of the people who sold produce and played drums on Congo Square. At twelve, she was baptized in the Mississippi River, where heavy Delta spirits washed over her. She recognized a good blues moan when she heard it. It's no coincidence that Willie Mae listened closely to Mahalia (and other Dorsey affiliates) or that Herbert Brewster was one of the thought leaders who built a home for Mahalia's voice. Willie Mae was made up of rich sources, and Brewster, Jackson, and Willie Mae herself were all sources tapped by Presley.

There were times when Mahalia was condemned by churchgoing folk for shouting the gospel. The volume of her voice and the bolting praise she amplified on the mic agitated restrictive cultural respectability politics. Mahalia, a shouter, was the heart of the Black gospel circuit in the '50s and '60s. Willie Mae, another shouter, was the heart of Texas R&B in the same period. Mahalia Jackson and Willie Mae were peers in their influence on regional sounds and national Black music movements — one hailed as god's music, the other as the devil's.

Recently, I made an emotionally charged decision. I filed my Mahalia Jackson records in my second-wave blueswomen category, top left of my third shelf, between Willie Mae and Rosetta Tharpe. I placed Jackson in the category of blueswomen, which was blasphemous and done blatantly against her wishes. I also caused more trouble by mixing her a cappella vocals with house music to create my own Black queer spirituals. Mahalia would never approve, but it's complicated. Publicly she described the blues and secular music as "indecent." But by her own standards, Mahalia's voice was perfect for blues indecency. Willie Mae was indecent. Rosetta Tharpe was indecent. Saidiya Hartman offers indecent believers a room of their own. Affirming the complex personhood of Black women, she said, "at the very least, the wayward inhabited the structure of their contradictions without shame. One could attend a traditional church and believe deeply in the Lord, yet still choose to live and love in a variant manner." Hartman speaks to the place where religious raunchiness can exist.

When the self-proclaimed "King of Rock 'n' Roll" Little Richard was asked to share his influences, one of the first names to fly off his glossy lips was Mahalia Jackson. That's why I'm comfortable with Mahalia Jackson's placement on my third shelf. The status I gave her as a Christian blues-woman reminds me that Mahalia was one of the founding voices and performers of rock, before even Little Richard. She would shake her head and allow for the curls to fall against her face and swing it back when they got in her eyes — wild, like the average rocker. Mahalia's indecent voice was again displayed when she sang "Didn't It Rain" at the 1958 Newport Jazz Festival. Her reworking presents an R&B song with only a touch of god in the lyrics. LaVern Baker recorded a jump-blues dance-floor version on her gospel album *Precious Memories* in 1957. Rosetta Tharpe solidified her status as a rock 'n' roll goddess when she covered the song for angsty British teenagers in Manchester in 1964. A trifecta of Black femme gospel rock.

In the 1997 documentary *Mahalia Jackson: The Power and the Glory*, close friends of the singer shared that she would secretly listen to the blues, which is to say that the blues were one of the secrets to her gospel success. But the secret broke loose every time she opened her mouth. She told close associates (I imagine in a kind of whisper) that Bessie Smith's moaning moved her. Mahalia Jackson was drawn to indecency. In 1971, she was in the final stage of her life as a performer. While on tour in Germany, she fell ill and was flown back to Chicago to recover. She died on January 27, 1972. Willie Mae, having spent years injecting samples from spirituals into her blues and R&B music, gathered her notes and created *Saved*, a thirty-minute funk-rock gospel album, in Mahalia's last living year.

Saved is secularized by the electric guitar, and Willie Mae's voice is colored by gin, tobacco, and hard blues joy. Not much about its sound can be judged by the album cover, which features a powder blue background with a small band of palm trees at the center. It could be Florida. It could be Nigeria. The word *Saved* is written above the scene in what appears to be wet paint spelled out with a finger. Above the album title is Willie Mae's name in all caps. The album is a return to her roots—the time before she graced the stage of the Apollo and left Harlem for the next city with her new stage name in tow. This was Willie Mae Thornton, George Thornton's and Mattie Haynes's daughter, and the full circle sound is clear. When I dropped the needle on the record, I was transported to a new Willie Mae realm. The album is complete with epic intros, interludes, and outros. There are handclaps to accentuate the faith, and there is freedom from compositional structure. Syncopation and radical imagination lead the way.

Willie Mae employs lyrical freestyles that spell out her connection to the Black church in a network of seemingly unrelated sounds. She was ready for this. Twenty seconds into the first song on the album is a slow-building avalanche of bongos, congas, electric keys, and wind chimes. Gradually the funk bubble is busted open by a chorus of soulful singers who arrive together on the one with the words "Oh happy day!" The Edwin Hawkins Singers released "Oh Happy Day" in 1968. Willie Mae's decision to open the album with it is like a secret announcement to Black church listeners who appreciate new twists on gospel standards. The truth is, "Oh Happy Day" was written in 1744 by a British clergyman named Philip Doddridge. By virtue of the year it was made, the song is rooted in the institution of slavery, yet it found international acclaim when Hawkins's version made its way to number 1 on the singles charts in the United States, France, Germany, the Netherlands, Canada, and Ireland. This means the start of Willie Mae's album is full of Black, British, and American history, and as unsavory as that history is, she changed how we heard the song by shifting the context from the globalized soulful gospel cover that Hawkins produced to an experimental acid rock version.

In "Down by the Riverside," we get psychedelic Blackness. It's theatrical (reeking of the musical *Hair*) and shows off the wide collection of ideas she drew from to build on the gospel tradition. It demonstrates the limitless shapes that gospel can take, particularly when you've been listening to it closely for fifty years and it was the very first music you heard. Then, on top of the layers of the song, we get a sermon in the middle. The instruments fade and the guitar and piano creep underneath her voice until all the sounds disappear to bring the song to an end. "Glory, Glory Hallelujah" features the piano and the Hammond B3 organ, a Black church staple. It has a blues swing enhanced by a persistent full drum kit, but I couldn't determine if Willie Mae was on the drums as there is so little information on this album. It's danceable gospel music, complete with a well-directed choir.

Willie Mae's version of "He's Got the Whole World" embodies a basic but soulful twist. The electric guitars are present, and the chorus holds up another improvisational mid-song sermon: "That man sticks by you when you don't know / He watches over you while you're sleeping / He watched you when you walking down the street." It's a Sunday school–friendly joint. The song "Lord Save Me" breaks into yet another improvisational sermon about being from Alabama, reinforcing what Black theologist James A. Cone meant when he said, "The spirituals were communicative devices about the possibilities of earthly freedom." To that end, Willie Mae sings, "In this land / I wish you would lift me up / 'Cause I can't run away / I gotta stay until you have your say / Lord, ain't that wonderful?" displaying her personal relationship with God. "Go Down Moses" is another dramatized old Negro spiritual. A sorrow song with mobilizing power and coded messaging that issued a call to move away from suffering. Willie Mae leads the congregation with hymn lining (speaking the lyrics before the choir sings them). Surprisingly, in her version, a classical piano sound meets traditional Baptist gospel music.

Perhaps one of the most dramatic introductions on

Saved comes on "Swing Low, Sweet Chariot." The conversation between the guitar and piano is most pronounced and only interrupted when the choir enters. This is another old Negro spiritual with a dynamic history. At Fisk University, my alma mater, students were told that the first recording of "Swing Low, Swing Chariot" was performed by the Fisk Jubilee Singers in 1909. This remains a source of pride for the university, and the Jubilee Singers perform the song worldwide to this day. My introduction to the song was Parliament's decision to reboot the chorus for their 1975 song "Mothership Connection (Star Child)," introducing a new generation of listeners to the spiritual. Notably, when Parliament performed it live in concert, they used it to signal the landing of their opulent, stage-friendly Mothership. The band's connecting of space and so-called heaven in a post-slavery context forms its own cosmology. The original Mothership is now exhibited at the Smithsonian National Museum of African American History and Culture. In 1992, a new iteration of the song was introduced to another generation when G-funk pioneer Dr. Dre sampled P "Mothership Connection" for the song "Let Me Ride" on *The Chronic* album. Willie Mae, while part of a lineage of Black folk who have their way with songs that tie them to the ghosts of bondage, uses "Swing Low, Sweet Chariot" as a personal testament and brings the wisdom of her mother and father into the lyrics.

Saved, which I've determined is my favorite Willie Mae album, is a thirty-minute love letter to her career, her family, and the places she calls home. It centered on her faith that she survived despite the sometimes-troubled journey. On this album, she stretches gospel, stretches the blues, and stretches Blackness, rendering ridiculous the binary of god's music and the devil's music. The only other reference I have that compares to *Saved* is *The Gospel According to Ike and Tina*, released in 1974, a peer in its ambitious use of Black R&B-rock as a tool to explore stories of endurance in the name of Jesus. Ike and Tina and Willie Mae brought blues ministry to life and, with it, a unique articulation of what Cone theorizes as "secular spirituals." Integrating these forces does not require you to choose between so-called good and evil. Instead, Willie Mae Thornton, a prideful seeker of alcoholic pleasure and fierce critic of the system that created national heartbreak for Black people, showed the blues what it meant to "have a talk with God" through song. This album is also a testament to all the mothering that made her the mother of *Saved*, one of the most important children in her body of work.

Mahalia Jackson helped mother Aretha Franklin—not symbolically, but practically and literally. Jackson was a regular fixture in Aretha's Detroit home when her father, the Reverend C. L. Franklin, needed support following Aretha's mother's death in 1952. Vocally, Aretha grew up watching Mahalia's godly grasp on singing, phrasing, and composing music. A year before Mahalia's death, Aretha was firmly established on the throne as the most soulful of Black music queens. After a lengthy career recording jazz, soul, and the blues, she pivoted to her sanctified roots. She dressed elegantly for a filmed two-day recording affair at New Temple Missionary, James Cleveland's Watts-based Baptist church. Cleveland (a mentee of Thomas Dorsey) was Aretha's musical play cousin. When Cleveland left Chicago, the two shared a home and lived with the Franklins in Detroit for a stint in the '50s. Those two days, January 13 and 14, 1972, produced the best-selling gospel album in the history of American music, *Amazing Grace*. Thirteen days later Mahalia Jackson died, and Aretha Franklin sang at her funeral. In March 1972, Willie Mae was called back to Europe.

When Willie Mae accepted an offer to join the next cohort of American Folk Blues Festival musicians—Eddie Boyd, Big Joe Williams, Robert Pete Williams, T-Bone Walker, Paul Lenart, Hartley Severns, Edward Taylor, and Vinton Johnson—were already onboard. This time she traveled to Germany, France, Italy, Switzerland, Holland, Austria, Denmark, Norway, and Finland. According to Spörke, Herbie Hancock happened to be in one of the countries where she performed and met up with the group of legends. I wonder what Herbie Hancock thought about her version of "Watermelon Man" and how she took it on a different path with humorous, culturally coded lyrics.

I was struck by a comment made by a fellow performer about Willie Mae. Paul Lenart described Willie Mae as having a reputation for being hard on fellow musicians in Spörke's biography. During the '72 American Folk Blues Festival, however, Lenart shared with Spörke that "she was not that way with us at all." I can only surmise that she was easier on these musicians because they were Black blues people and she felt no need to protect the music. After a run of successful live shows, the recording of *Saved*, television appearances, and blues festivals, Willie Mae returned to the studio and recorded two more albums that solidified her status as one of history's greatest blues artists. More impressive was her ability to demonstrate blues music as an omnipresent force in all genres of Black music.

A *JAILED SASSY* MAMA

How and why, then, did California go about the biggest prison-building project in the history of the world?

RUTHIE GILMORE

My mother cursed a lot, and she could dance. I used to watch her hips and smile, knowing she was there to teach me deep groove — the workings of Black rhythm science. What I know is that some women are chosen by music *and* captured by the system. My mother spent time in Cali jails and prisons. Back and forth to court. In and out of our lives. My grandmother, protectively, told me that Mama was sick in the hospital. Years later, I discovered she meant caged for her addiction. Nothing rehabilitative. Everything punitive. Willie Mae cursed a lot, and she could dance. She, too, spent time in Cali jails and prisons — sometimes caged for her addiction — in real life, as a live performer, and fictionally through lyrics.

More than a framework, Sarah Haley's book *No Mercy Here: Gender, Punishment, and the Making of Jim Crow Modernity* offers far-reaching theoretical care. Haley's combing through the archives of Black women in Georgia state prisons in the nineteenth and twentieth centuries helped me unpack the politics of refusal embedded in Willie Mae's voice and my mother's hips. The book interrogates "the development of systems of terror, structures of economic and political subordination, and hidden dimensions of working-class African American women's lives." As a DJ, daughter of a formerly incarcerated mother, and student of Willie Mae's life, I am moved by this scholarly blend. My proximity to the prisons and systems of terror Haley describes makes her work invaluable to the project of learning the intricacies that exist between Black music, Black women, and prisons — and where Willie Mae and my mother fit in the story.

Willie Mae wasn't the first Black woman to use the blues to call out the carceral system. Many women artists before and after her — across generation and genre — railed against the ever-present role of prisons in their lives. These musical sounds of resistance show up along with critical developments in the prison system. Haley explains, "From 1908 until 1936, black women were virtually the only female prisoners on the chain gang." This period coincides with an explosion of prison-themed blues from blueswomen. In *Black Pearls*, Daphne Duval Harrison speaks to the conditions that put the prison blues in motion: "The image of the vengeful woman who acted out her violence is often cast in a prison setting." "Courthouse Blues" (1924–25) by Clara Smith, "Sing Sing Prison" and "Jailhouse Blues" (1924–25) by Bessie Smith, and "Worried Jailhouse Blues" (1946) by Bertha Chippier Hill recount the horrid conditions of prison life and their toll on one's physical and mental well-being. Clara Smith considers a three-month sentence light compared to how the man she loved made her feel — "ninety-nine years old." Though she was jailed "on account of one trifling man," the jury acquitted her.

A rare performance supports Harrison's analysis. In 1929, Mamie Smith appeared in the short film *Jailhouse Blues*, produced by Columbia Pictures. In the movie, Mamie visits a prison and sings about the loss of her elusive lover. She's heartbroken by his frequent arrests: "I have a no-good man who loves the jail so much / He stays in jail all the time." A few years before this Hollywood production Bessie Smith sang a similar tune. Some of her earliest recordings (1923–28) reference jail as casually as they did her love for no-good men. Bessie's version of "Jailhouse Blues" hints at her subversive desire for other women in the prison setting: "Thirty days in jail with my back turned to the wall / Turned to the wall / Thirty days in jail with my back turned to the wall / Look here, Mr. Jailkeeper, put another gal in my stall." Bessie Smith managed to find joy in her captivity, and Haley reads this "desire fulfilled by another woman" as being "the only punctuation on her long sentence."

While most blueswomen sang from inside heterosexual relationships that pushed them to snap, Willie Mae's target was the system itself. In "Unlucky Girl" (1968), Willie Mae sings about how her relationship with alcohol is hindered by the FBI and police who follow her. She is arrested and "back in jail" for enjoying her liquor: "The old folks told me drinking was killing poor me / But I told the old folk I can't help it / Whiskey won't let me be / How unlucky / How unlucky can an ol' girl be / I gotta keep on drinking my gin / But the FBI is following me." Willie Mae was unashamed of her relationship with alcohol and uncomfortably close to the prison system. Her references to jail, the FBI, the police, and Ronald Reagan reflect lived experiences. I mentioned in a previous chapter how her version of "Funky Broadway" adds lyrics in which the singer and her friends are partying too loudly, leading to a group arrest. This meta-commentary reveals her constant awareness of the state's reach into Black life. In her essay titled "'New Bones' Abolitionism, Communism, and Captive Maternals," Abolitionist scholar Joy James names prisons as "the most tangible domestic war zone." In her music, Willie Mae Thornton takes up arms on the war's front line.

There are no songs in Willie Mae's catalog about a man she lost to prison, nor are there songs about going to jail behind a man she loved to hate or hated to love. Yet references to prisons, judges, police, and state officials are persistent throughout her catalog and live performances. How much of her encounters with the cops can be linked to her gender presentation? It's easy to believe that Willie Mae experienced layers of discriminatory policing and excessive force because of how she performed gender. This might explain how her prison and police blues differ from those of other blueswomen. Close listeners of Willie Mae's music must reckon with her soulful articulation of the perceived criminality of Black people, namely herself. Further, she used the recording industry to critique the state. In this way, her recordings and lyrical resistance toward policing were sabotaging the music industry's customarily apolitical stance.

Haley's work highlights the "black radical tradition" of sabotage and asserts that "both the narrow and expansive meanings of sabotage describe the actions of imprisoned women and black female artists' depictions of imprisonment and the law: the resources that they disrupted were

material and ideological." I maintain that the music industry operates as an extension of the sharecropping economic model. Willie Mae's artful sabotage was manifested
in her using her platform to discuss politics. Taking advan-
tage of the resources of the music industry, built on the
exploited labor of Black people for centuries, Willie Mae
amplified her message to the communities who were most
vulnerable to the abuses of both the carceral system and
the recording industry itself. Willie Mae's work was part
of what Haley calls a "sonic radical blues tradition."

American prisons have always tucked away rageful
Black women, constructing steel nests to contain their
flames. Willie Mae Thornton was a Sagittarius — the element of fire was part of her DNA. Fiery Black women in
America burn at both ends. What was it like to be close to
her fire? Did it burn when she asked for equal pay? Did she
suffer for her righteous fury and comedic defiance? The
answers to these questions are a simple yes. She fought
physically and musically, publicly and privately, literally
and figuratively, against dirty cops, cheating promoters,
and shady record company executives. As mentioned in a
prior chapter, she was arrested and then blacklisted from
several clubs in the Bay Area. She was known to act unpre-
dictably when the explosive combination of alcohol, unsavory business deals, and personal encounters with social
injustice blocked her path. She saw the humor (or ridicu-
lousness) in her interactions with the law and made them
part of her act.

Returning to Willie Mae's introduction on *The Way It Is*
(1970) is crucial to understanding how she dealt with police
violence. The album, recorded live at a venue called Thee
Experience in Los Angeles in 1969, opens with her telling

the crowd about an arrest the night before in LA: "Out of all the places I've been, Europe and all over the United States, and a dumb cop come up last night and said I stole a gun, charged me for robbery, and I ain't never stole nothing in my life." It's unclear if this is part of her act or if it really happened. She continues her complaint against the LAPD, but in reporting, she takes a shot at the cop for the nature of the charge: "Why I'ma rob somebody? I make more money than he make in one year . . . in one night, now I'm going around and gon' steal something? But I got news for him, I'm gonna tell the world about that." From there, she introduces and performs "Little Red Rooster."

Typically, when I've heard Black people say "I got news for you" over the last forty-seven years of my life, it referred to a possible plan of action leading to some iteration of justice or revenge. Some unexpected twist that will make it so that enemies or opponents will somehow pay for the transgression at hand. By threatening that she's "gonna tell the world," Willie Mae is admitting that her platform, the live recording she knew would be made widely available through music industry distribution, is where she could assert her innocence in the court of public opinion. Of course, in a real court of law, asserting her innocence and insulting the state would be much more difficult.

Willie Mae performs a version of "Watermelon Man" on the same live album. She launches into her imaginary exchange with a hustling watermelon man—that it's a Herbie Hancock track she's redefining with theatricality and vaudevillian flair is part of the magic. In the song, Willie Mae notices that the watermelon man is overcharging her for the fruit, and so she threatens to call the police.

The threat, however, feels less about reporting someone for a minor cultural infraction (overpriced watermelon) and more about how the minor infraction could turn into an unwarranted arrest from overzealous cops willing to answer the call. She doesn't trust the cops, and she's conscious of their ongoing harassment, but she is ready to include them when, in her negotiation process, things escalate.

"And if you sell me a watermelon for my five dollars / It's got to be my size." When he sticks to the price she takes it up a notch: "You ain't got no license for here in my driveway, so move your truck / I'll call the police and they'll take you to jail like they did me / And they don't even eat watermelon / Ah, you gon' be so smart about it, I'll call Ronald Reagan / I'll get one free then, you gon' sell him one? / What? / Look man, Ronald Reagan don't play like that."

Willie Mae references Reagan as the omnipresent law-and-order enforcer. She's clear, though, that neither Reagan nor the cops are the kind of people who eat watermelon. In this exchange, there's a reclamation. Watermelon is upheld as a Black American delicacy, and the history of it being weaponized as a stereotype is rejected by her shameless tactics to procure one at a reasonable price. Through her lyrics and unscripted performance, Willie Mae communicates the value of the fruit and the secret meaning it maintains in Black communities. Her commentary positions those unfamiliar with the importance of watermelon as a threat to Black freedom, aligned with police brutality and state violence.

Prison themes in music are not limited to the blues. Many artists recorded live albums in prison, Johnny Cash's

At San Quentin (1969) being among the most famous. I was less surprised to learn about bluesmen who recorded prison albums like *Live in Cook County Jail* by B. B. King (1971) and *Live at Soledad Prison* by John Lee Hooker (1972) but more surprised to learn that the reggae band Black Uhuru performed at Soledad Prison in 1982 (a little more than a decade after the infamous prison yard riots and the death/assassination of George Jackson) and that the Sex Pistols recorded a prison album, *Live at Chelmsford Top Security Prison*, at a UK facility in 1976. These blues, reggae, and punk prison performances make sense in the context of the anti-government sentiments those genres often express; but as with the public discourse that centers the mass incarceration of Black men, I was left to ask, where are the women and their prison albums?

Willie Mae was among an elite group of Black women, along with the comedians Moms Mabley and Mo'Nique, to perform in jails or prisons. Their combined stories and collective bodies of work shrunk the gap between the imprisoned and their communities of origin. Moms Mabley released her *Live at Sing Sing* album in 1971. Willie Mae released *Jail* in 1975. In 2007 Mo'nique released a film and album recording of her stand-up performance at Ohio Reformatory for Women aptly titled *I Could Have Been Your Cellmate!* It's no coincidence that Willie Mae, Mo'Nique, and Moms Mabley found themselves entertaining the American imprisoned, as each is known for their unique brand of raunchiness that could be classified as criminal. It's a raunchiness typically associated with a working-class Black performance poetics. But there's another, more disturbing connector at play, it's what happens in the time between Moms Mabley's and Mo'Nique's albums.

Between 1970 and 2007, America began its mass incarceration era. The Vera Institute reports that women were the fastest growing correctional population in the country, increasing fourteen-fold between 1970 and 2014. The Vera Institute names how "women are particularly vulnerable to the harms of incarceration for several reasons: the majority of women in custody have experienced trauma, have unmet mental and physical health needs, are single mothers, and come from low-income communities of color." Indeed, Moms Mabley, Willie Mae, and Mo'Nique *Could Have Been Cellmates!* of the people they performed for in so-called correctional facilities, jails, and prisons.

I'm especially fond of one-word album titles: Sade's *Promise*, Santana's *Abraxas*, and Aretha's *Sparkle* come to mind. Willie Mae's *Jail* is a one-word album title that communicates the profound, matter-of-fact nature of prisons in the lives of Black people. The *Jail* album was bound up with the experiences of Black women, though she performs for imprisoned men. Her show for the men is generous in that her solidarity does more than offer an empty gesture. The sincerity is in the recorded performance. Her generosity is a testament to what could happen to Willie Mae once she steps outside the prison doors. Willie Mae, in all aspects of the word, knew this audience. The thin line between the inside and outside for Black people is sonically and socially apparent.

Willie Mae's *Jail* combines two concerts at Monroe State Prison in Washington State and Oregon State Reformatory in Eugene. It opens with her making the mistake of saying "ladies and gentlemen," a moment that could easily create tension in the room. Instead, Willie Mae hints at the fact that she's used to addressing a mixed crowd; before she launches into her instrumental, she corrects the record and says, "Menz and all, and whatnot," and the place erupts in laughter. Whether the responses from the men are real is arguable. In his biography on Willie Mae, Spörke spoke to how the men created a chilly environment when Willie Mae performed and the audience response was manipulated in post-production. After her introduction, she begins an up-tempo R&B version of "Little Red Rooster," again flexing her range. Notably, before singing any lyrics, she blows the harmonica and continues to blow for most of the song. Next is "Ball 'n' Chain." Unsurprisingly, she acknowledges that Janis popularized the song. Willie Mae brought Joplin into the state facility. This rendition is a slow groove that has added blaring horns. The space between her words builds enough tension for the men to talk to her throughout the song in a call-and-response fashion: "Yes ma'am, tell it, Big Mama." They may see themselves (and hear their voices, which were scattered throughout the album to compensate for their limited engagement) in Willie Mae. Many men in prison could relate to being down on luck but sober with unbreakable dignity.

The song "Jail" provides insight into Willie Mae's primary concern with prison: "Well, here I am again / Sitting down in this old rotten jail." Yes, there is violence and inhumane treatment of prisoners, but her biggest problem is wasted time. Simply stating that jail is a waste of time is essential here. It's a radical perspective to hold when you consider how much time Black people and their families have lost to prisons. "I looked next door in the cell," she sings, "I said brother, how much time do you have?" Another question arises from this moment in the song. Is she (her protagonist) in a men's or a co-ed facility? Or is she simply catering to the crowd? When her cellmate answers,

"He said I got five long years," you hear the imprisoned men in the audience whistle in agreement, assuming that studio engineers did not manufacture that response. Willie Mae (in the song) then returns to her experience: "Sitting here, baby, wasting time / I say I got ninety-nine years to go / And I know it's one day," meaning she's only served one day so far. Willie Mae repeats, "Sitting in jail ain't nothing but a waste of time." Seconds after the last word is sung, the band bursts into funkified versions of "Hound Dog" and "Rock Me Baby," which she again leads with the harmonica and is joined by an extended saxophone solo.

The song "Sheriff O.E. and Me" again calls attention to the presence of cops, but it's more of a country-folk blues, and she offers another impressive harmonica solo. After pausing for a moment, she introduces the song's first lyrics: "Sitting at home, minding my own / A man came up to my door / I peeped through the screen / He looked tall and mean / He had a leg .44 / He said Sheriff O.E., you know me / . . . / Sitting at home, minding my own." The key words in the songs are "sitting at home." Hence, whether she's at the club being arrested ("Funky Broadway"), being arrested for stealing a gun ("Little Red Rooster"), or sitting at home, minding her own ("Sheriff O.E. and Me"), Willie Mae is under constant threat of police harassment. Her final song is "Oh Happy Day," a hopeful exit. For this song, it sounds as if the men in the audience are clapping along. Her ad-libs highlight a cross between funk and faith. She shouts and pivots from the original lyrics to throw in new words. The tempo increases in the last thirty seconds, and the emcee returns to the stage to introduce Willie Mae as she exits. Her work is done.

Jail broke a four-year recording dry spell. The full circle moment begins with her performance at the Jazz in the

Garden series at New York's Museum of Modern Art in 1971. By 1975 Ed Bland, who curated the MoMA shows, was head of A&R at Vanguard Records. He not only secured Willie Mae as a Vanguard artist but also made it possible for her to release shows that had been recorded during her Pacific Northwest tour in 1971 in which she shared the bill with Muddy Waters, George "Harmonica" Smith, and Joe Turner among others. He also exercised a considerable amount of control over her Vanguard recordings. In Willie Mae's biography, Bland is quoted as saying "I was in charge of the musicians' union contracts and the publishing info. Needless to say, I was in charge of the album concept, the artwork, and the determination of the musical qualities and the sonic qualities of the recordings." I find it curious that Bland states that it's needless to say he was in control of every aspect of the recording process. Given the racialized power difference between Thornton and Bland, and the unsavory exploitive history of the American music industry and men who control the careers of women, I am left to wonder how much power Willie Mae was forced to give up—particularly the determination of the musical qualities he claims to have controlled—when she signed with Vanguard.

Bland also shares that Willie Mae was easy to work with when she was sober and "as long as one was straight with her money. . . . She also liked the musicians I selected to play with her. And she got her money promptly." What's striking about this statement is that yet again we are missing Willie Mae's voice in the telling of her story. Bland's statement leaves little room for any complaint or concern Willie Mae might have had. Nevertheless, the other album she recorded for Vanguard in 1975, *Sassy Mama*, is another top-notch performance, though that's not the album I want to review. There are two *Sassy Mama* albums. The one released by Vanguard in 1975 and a live version. I am most moved by the live version recorded at the Rising Sun Celebrity Jazz Club in Montreal on April 12, 1977, and released by the Canadian based label Just a Memory in 1994. It includes several of the songs originally recorded for the Vanguard release and a few others she performs just for the audience. She does a few things on this album that need to be named.

It could be argued that this performance of *Sassy Mama* is Willie Mae's Black rock album. Upon first listening, I kept referring back to Jimi Hendrix and the live 1969 album he recorded with the all-Black Band of Gypsys. In a 1973 rockumentary film simply titled *Jimi Hendrix*, Hendrix's ex-girlfriend, the late Lithofayne Pridgon (also known as Fayne Pridgon), described the role of the blues in Hendrix's listening practice: "There was a time when he was heavy heavy heavy into blues. Blues was it. He'd play a little rock every now and then a little R&B but it was stomp down funky blues. Elmore James was his favorite, he used to take his hotel glasses and put it on the string and you know like they'd do those steel bars and get that sound that Elmore gets. . . . 'The Sky Is Crying' was his favorite. 'It Hurts Me Too' was a favorite of his, but 'The Sky is Crying' was his main thing." *Sassy Mama* convinces me that Hendrix was born out of the blues, and Willie Mae's mothering, fathering, and ungendering of the blues helps me understand the sound of *Sassy Mama* as representative of a kind of midwifery of both Black rock and Hendrix himself.

Several moments in the album deserve close review. The album title is drawn from a song written by Mattie

Fields, Willie Mae's younger sister (same father, different mother), who acted as both her caretaker and informal manager throughout the seventies. The words Willie Mae uses to start the album are "You know I wasn't ready to go on, but we got three shows to do tonight, so, I might as well go on and do my little bit." This song, titled "Tell Me Pretty Baby," is the one that reminds me most of the Band of Gypsys. The way she rides over the rhythm guitar and curates the performance is reminiscent of how Hendrix talks over the driving drum and bass. Hendrix's commentary ranges from sharp critique of the Vietnam War, like on the song "Machine Gun," to publicly sharing songwriting credit with his bandmates. I'm also convinced that this album's performance of "Ball 'n' Chain" might be my favorite. In the introduction she does her usual spiel: "I wrote this song, ladies and gentlemen, in 1960, and the late and great Janis Joplin, she asked me could she do it, so I told her yes. But I had the pleasure of putting it on record before she did. So here it is, in my own way, the way I wrote it. And she might have did some changes, I don't know." Willie Mae knows for sure that Big Brother and the Holding Company changed it and had more commercial success than she did, but she continues, "Now see, I can't sing like nobody but me. I might sing your song, but no way in the world I can do you. Alright, fellas D minor, slow and easy, take it low, B. B. King style." She assigns King his own genre of blues while hinting at the fact that Joplin's version was good but not the full truth of the song. Willie Mae reinforces sonically that the original is born of generations of Black musical traditions. In this way, "Ball 'n' Chain" has been returned to sender.

Other songs on the album, like "Watermelon Man" and

"Rock Me Baby," are more of her standards. She also does something interesting with how she blends tunes. "Hound Dog" is mixed with "Walkin' the Dog," and "Sweet Little Angel" is mixed with "Three O'clock Blues," demonstrating her deep intimacy with the blues as a system of recall, recycling, and memory. This album also includes Willie Mae's version of "Summertime." While the album is uneventful in terms of the selection of songs, there is a sonic quality that secures her a position as a Black rock influencer and, like Little Richard and Mahalia Jackson, an architect of American rock 'n' roll.

For centuries, Black people have managed another rational fear—the hospital blues. The American medical industry is part of the structural racism and systems of terror that Haley points to in *No Mercy Here* and that Saidiya Hartman recounts in her poetic framing of legacies of slavery, *Lose Your Mother: A Journey along the Atlantic Slave Route*. Hartman names the afterlife of slavery as "skewed life chances, limited access to health and education, premature death, incarceration, and impoverishment." With Hartman's analysis in mind, I can understand why, even when she lost several hundred pounds (dropping from 350 to 95 pounds in a short amount of time), Willie Mae may have had trouble trusting hospitals with her health. Between 1975 and 1976, Willie Mae was diagnosed with cancer. Even before the diagnosis, doctors warned her to stop touring and drinking before her body finally succumbed to stresses of her lifestyle.

To be clear, hers was not the rock 'n' roll fantasy of sex, drugs, and excessive money. This was a working-class blues lifestyle of appearing at small clubs for low pay to pay rent and buy groceries. Throughout her career, Willie

Mae stayed with friends and family. She also stayed in apartments, boarding homes, and hotel rooms. I imagine how knowing the difference between a lifestyle of white excess — built on the appropriation or incorporation of the blues and other Black musical forms — and your own lifestyle of struggle as an innovative artist could lead to heavy drinking. She was battling, at once, a social illness and a terminal illness inside her body.

In 1977, when Elvis died, Willie Mae was quoted in Spörke's biography as saying "Look at all he had, and he's dead and gone and I'm still here." To seal the indifference she added, "Last time I was in Memphis they told me, 'We lost so and so,' I said did you find him?" I believe that these words reflect, in the spirit of James Brown, a kind of payback blues. Her comments, perceived as cruel by some, had a hint of Malcolm X's well-known response to Kennedy's assassination: "Chickens coming home to roost never did make me sad, they've always made me glad." Malcolm was speaking about a culture of violence defined and upheld by the American presidency. Willie Mae was speaking about the culture of theft defined and upheld by the American music industry. Malcolm felt like the urgency of his cause (Pan-African solidarity against US-led global white supremacy) was affirmed by the assassination of Kennedy. Willie Mae felt vindicated by the circumstances of Presley's death and how they brought attention to her resilience. She saw the passing of "so and so" as a clearing of debt, and she was willing to name the irony of it, *by any means necessary*.

THE '80S BLACKNESS OF WILLIE MAE'S BLUES

One of my favorite things about Willie Mae is that she traveled with a hot plate and cooked chitlins in her hotel room while on tour. She did this to the chagrin of hotel guests and fellow band members. This, too, was part of her politics of refusal. She knew Black Americans were careful about when and where they cleaned and cooked chitlins. That we found private joy in the ritual around the vicious little scraps we were given. Innovation out of hardship. A Chitlin' Circuit of possibility. The smell of chitlins, then, is political too. A reminder of where the blues come from — we, the witnesses of slavery. Black people were given the least desirable part of the pig while working the fields. I was introduced to chitlins as a soul food staple in the 1980s. I'm not a witness of slavery, but I witnessed what chitlins did to my grandmother's and her mother's body. Chitlins, like the blues, smell like Black creativity in the face of white supremacy.

June 19, 1979, was an important day for all Black people and for Willie Mae Thornton in particular. She was invited back to Texas to celebrate its Juneteenth festivities. Originating in Galveston, Texas, Juneteenth commemorates the ending of slavery in the United States. The enslavement of Black Texans carried on for two years after

Lincoln penned the Emancipation Proclamation, abolishing slavery, in 1863. And even when the news of so-called freedom arrived on June 19, 1865, the conditions of slavery were reinvented through other sinister social devices like the codification of Black criminality and the creation of a prison system to catch the coded bodies. This stunning moment in history set the stage for Willie Mae's performance at the annual Juneteenth Blues Festival in Texas, though there is no record of her appearance. Founded by pianist, composer, educator, and jazz festival promoter Lanny Steele, the Juneteenth Blues Festival was one of very few music festivals produced by Black people. Willie Mae performed there in 1978 and 1979. She began her end-of-life journey by revisiting the history she created around her music. The state of Texas is a Willie Mae Thornton historical landmark and the site of delayed freedom.

When rap music reached commercial status in 1979 with the Sugarhill Gang's "Rapper's Delight," a tune that highlighted the emergent culture of looping and sampling with its use of Chic's disco-funk classic "Good Times." Willie Mae was based on the West Coast moving between residencies in Los Angeles clubs like the Partisan Room and the Rubaiyat Room. By the early '80s, Willie Mae was still active, like many blues elders. She appeared at a series of concerts and events largely financed by white enthusiasts built around themes of nostalgia (oldies but goodies as a genre) and novelty (blueswomen). But the blues, her blues, were always relevant, always alive. Never was Willie Mae Thornton a has-been. Prestigious opportunities were scarcer, and it was clear that was not going to reach the commercial status she had hoped for. But she was a beloved force in the blues, R&B, folk, rock, gospel, and jazz community—having in some way or another, shaped or been shaped by all those genres.

Willie Mae continued performing with her comrades George "Harmonica" Smith, Joe Turner, Muddy Waters, and other giants like B. B. King and John Lee Hooker. These alliances solidified her status as a peer to the men history treats as pure blues artists. Hazel Carby explains how the "field of blues history is dominated by the assumption that 'authentic' blues forms are entirely rural in origin and are produced by the figure of the wandering lone male." Yet, forty years after she left Alabama as a wandering lone woman, Willie Mae was still pushing the music, whether the traditional blues were at the forefront of the Black American musical imagination or on the edges of its ancestral memory.

On July 2, 1980, Willie Mae Thornton performed at the "Blues Is a Woman" segment of the Newport Jazz Festival, organized by Rosetta Reitz, a white feminist jazz historian and Black blueswoman ally. She started Rosetta Records in 1970 and centered the *Foremothers*, *Big Mamas*, and *Super Sisters* (compilation titles from her collection) from the 1920s through the 1960s. She was famous for literally diggin' through the crates—78s no less—and discovering lost music available in the public domain. Honorably, she searched for the owner of the rights to the music to pay royalties to those still living or their families. Reitz made the music and, therefore the women, available to a larger audience. She described the power of the blueswomen to the *Christian Science Monitor*: "They hired the musicians and the chorus line, a lot of them wrote the music themselves, and they produced their shows. They were more than just singers; they were symbols of success."

I first learned of Reitz's work through Hazel Carby, who writes with admiration about Rosetta Records' detailed liner notes. In her essay "They Put a Spell on You," Carby described Reitz's records as being "the most indispensable resource for introducing students to the blues women and their music. . . . Each record is accompanied by liner notes which are well researched and more informative than any books currently available." Granted, there's been a considerable amount of blues scholarship produced by Black women since the time of Carby's writing in the late '80s, but the conviction of her belief at that time gives credibility to Reitz's efforts.

Programming for the 1980 Newport Jazz Festival was the natural progression of Rosetta Records. Reitz approached festival organizer George Wein with the idea to honor the women who contributed to the blues and, as such, the structure of jazz. The result was "Blues Is a Woman," and Willie Mae was part of the lineup for both years of its run. These performances demonstrate how Willie Mae walked over the threshold of a new decade and landed on her feet (even if sitting down). I listened to both shows since no video footage was available and enjoyed the task of figuring out the personality of each voice—a true listening practice complete with note-taking and researching the names and images of the women who were called to the stage.

The women present were heavyweights from across the blues spectrum. Carmen McRae was the mistress of ceremonies; also on stage were Adelaide Hall, a significant figure in the Harlem Renaissance who spent most of her seventy-year career between the US and the UK; Nell Carter, a multitalented Broadway and television actress; Koko Taylor, a Memphis-born Chicago-claimed "Queen of Blues"; Linda Hopkins, a New Orleans–born blues legend and Broadway actress discovered by Mahalia Jackson; Beulah Bryant, a lesser-known but equally fierce Alabama-born West Coast blues singer; Sharon Freeman, an instrumentalist, composer-pianist, and French horn player; and Sippie Wallace, a legendary blues singer, songwriter, and organist who performed (either on stage or in her beloved Detroit church) until her very last month of life. Like all the women chosen to participate, Willie Mae embodied the fact that blues is in fact a woman — and that there are many different ways to be a blueswoman.

McRae was a vibrant emcee who entwined herself between each performance, encouraging and applauding each musician/singer and educating the audience in the process: "The blues keep moving and changing, they have always been a living music, that's why we have so many different blues . . . country blues, city blues, folk blues, classic blues, low-down blues, high-tone vaudeville blues, guitar blues, piano blues, and big band blues. The blues is very basic to American music, blues is to jazz what yeast is to bread, [*crowd laughs*] can you dig it? Without it, it's flat." Carmen not only established the connection between blues and jazz but also communicated their musical interdependence.

Introducing Sippie Wallace, McRae described her as "an original, true-blue shouter of the golden era." Wallace says thank you to the crowd for what feels like no fewer than fifty times throughout her performance. Her gratitude is profound. She's a blues legend being given her flowers for fashioning, with her life, the stories that made Reitz's liner notes possible. Wallace signed a contract with

Okeh Records in 1929 and recorded the widely successful *Women Be Wise* album in 1966. Wallace, like Willie Mae, toured Europe as part of the American Folk Blues Festival cohort in 1966. Born in 1898, Sippie Wallace, in 1980, was living blues history.

In 1976, four years before the Newport Jazz Festival, Willie Mae began her recovery from a serious car accident. This incident highlights the parallels between Bessie Smith's and Willie Mae's lives. One of the tragedies that surround the blues is how Bessie Smith was said to have died. She was denied hospital treatment (hospital blues) after a car accident and didn't survive. The story behind Smith's death is contested in Jackie Kay's republished work *Bessie Smith: A Poet's Biography of a Blues Legend*, but nevertheless it's useful as a cautionary tale.

In her earlier years as a singer, before the "Big Mama" title, Willie Mae was called Little Bessie Smith by Black blues lovers who saw her perform in the '40s. Unlike Bessie, Willie Mae survived her car accident, though her injuries would leave her hospitalized for six months and in rehabilitation for the rest of her life. Upon being discharged, she used a wheelchair for mobility. Similar to Michael Jackson's 1993 appearance at the *Soul Train Music Awards*, where he pantomimed the choreography on stage in a chair while recovering from injuries, she performed her gigs and played harmonica while offering her own kind of chair dancing. Her determination was tenacious and audacious. Even with her ailing and aging body, the crowds were riled up by her sense of humor, her upper-body movement, and her face acting.

McRae's introduction of Willie Mae includes a brief list of her accomplishments. Shortly after the riotous applause,

Willie Mae speaks with a slight slur (from age and pain, not necessarily alcohol): "I would like to say thank you and thank everybody that is responsible for bringing me back here. And I hope you have enjoyed everyone that came in before me. I'm just now walking back. Six months of it now." Willie Mae takes this time to explain the accident: "I wish I could get up and perform like I used to, but I'm gon' do my best sitting down here." The silence between her words feels performative but sincere. She's pensive, honored to still be alive, honored to have been invited and to be performing, regardless of her body's public/private battle. The next sound you hear is her harmonica. At that moment, she becomes the one and only harmonica player in the lineup. For a brief second, Willie Mae stops playing to say, "You know I want to hear a little guitar, just a little bit." And then, "You know I was eight years old when I learned how to play this thing," referring to the harmonica.

Once the musicians are poised and ready, Willie Mae breaks out into a Black church pulpit "Rock-a-bye Baby" mini-sermon, making audible her parents' touch on her musical soul. Based on archival photos from this event, Willie Mae is wearing a full suit, and the brim of her cowboy hat frames a gaunt but joyful face. Her second number is the highly anticipated "Hound Dog." Before she sings it, she tells the crowd, "Right now, it's time for the one that I got robbed of called . . ."; without introducing its title, she simply lunges into the song, using her voice to signal a call to action by the musicians. The first five words, "You ain't nothing but a . . . ," are a cappella until the musicians drop in at the end of her last word. The words "hound dog" become the marker for when to enter. This version is a slow, dragging blues that matches the truth of the time she's spent working stages, clubs, and venues across America and Europe. "Hound Dog" is tired but still hers. When Carmen comes out to introduce Willie Mae again at the end of her performance, the crowd claps for close to a minute, prompting Carmen to ask, "It's still going on, isn't it? It's still tingling. Let us not forget to celebrate our living history, the women who keep the tradition alive."

To close 1980, Willie Mae performed on stage with Aretha Franklin for the *Omnibus* program on ABC, hosted by Hal Holbrook. In an interview before the performance, Aretha flexes her impressive knowledge of the history of Black music, sharing her thoughts on the importance of preserving the blues and particularly the work of Bessie Smith: "This song, that Bessie Smith first sang in 1929, may prove that the blues are indeed universal." Seconds later, the screen fades to black and Aretha and Willie Mae appear on stage. Willie Mae's biographer Michael Spörke shares an interesting take on the performance and on her condition at the time that could provide some insight into the sometimes contentious space between white biographers and the everyday lives of Black blues people: "Thornton had obviously not lost her strong will and still didn't like other female singers in her show. She didn't want to share the stage with Aretha Franklin, so she stomped up and down the dressing room. In fact, Thornton was just jealous of Franklin — and insecure." He doesn't share how he arrived at this conclusion, but I'm curious about other ways the moment can be read based on the performance alone.

I walked away with a different feeling upon seeing Willie Mae and Aretha together. In the banter they share before the song begins, Aretha says, "Alright Big Mama, tell me about it," and Willie Mae responds, "What you want me to do, Re." Throughout the song, they talk between riffs and runs. Aretha did not let everyone call her Re. She insisted that most people outside of her circle call her Ms. Franklin. Nicknames hold weight in Black communities, particularly when considering the history of violence and slavery attached to one's name. To take on another name, one you might have chosen or one your family might have chosen for you, is to be allowed to redefine your fate, to live up to your purpose, or to establish autonomy and essential boundaries. Martin Luther King referred to Aretha as Re, but Jerry Wexler and Clive Davis, at her request, called her Ms. Franklin until she felt ready for a different name, a different level of intimacy.

Next to Aretha, Willie Mae appeared frail, sitting in a chair on stage. She seemed aware of her limitations but available for the historic duet. During the performance, Aretha engages Willie Mae as an elderly queen deserving of respect. While there are moments when Aretha's voice soars over Willie Mae, the dignity in Willie Mae's eyes and the care in Aretha's gentle touch on Willie Mae's shoulder communicates a level of familiar/familial affection that Spörke might have missed. These two Black women share an understanding of what it means to have and then survive the blues. What I heard, saw, and felt was three different generations of blueswomen on stage, holding and honing the tradition—which is to say that Bessie Smith was summoned to the room by the collaborative effort of Willie Mae and Aretha. The Bessie song they sing, "Nobody Knows When Your Down," is the spiritual glue.

On March 23, 1983, Willie Mae performed as part of a televised PBS show titled, appropriately enough, *Three*

Generations of the Blues. The show featured Sippie Wallace (first gen), Willie Mae (second gen), and Jeannie Cheatham (third gen). According to Jeannie Cheatham, Willie Mae Thornton and Sippie Wallace didn't like each other and were surprised by the finale, which required them to appear on stage together. Again, I'm conscious of the tendency to engage women as being ready for a catfight. More frustrating is how I've yet to come across stories about bluesmen who didn't like each other. Spörke's read on the performance, based on his interview with Jeannie Cheatham, is that "the ninety-two-year-old vocalist Wallace, and the almost thirty-five years younger Thornton, starting trading verse after verse of made-up-on-the spot lyrics — insulting each other, each other's man and their mamas." Immediately upon reading this, I wondered about Spörke's relationship with the dozens and Cheatham's perspective that could be informed by generational differences. Was this truly public personal beef, or a professional "battle" common among Black musicians?

To warm up the crowd before her set, Willie Mae says to the crowd, "How is everybody? Is everybody alright? Yes, I wish I could say the same about me." She is weak in appearance but dressed sharp in a fuchsia muumuu with a matching beret. Underneath the muumuu are creased slacks and hard black shoes, like the kind a preacher would wear under his robe. Her strong voice rises from her long torso while she sings, using the strength from her diaphragm. Once she takes a seat on stage, less than five minutes after she arrives, her voice is even more robust. Willie Mae performs a smashing version of "Ball 'n' Chain," taking her time and stretching out the last lines in the song to match the reach of her career. Next, she performs "Hound

Dog" while holding her head high. There is no shame and no regret. Again, this is her song. In the middle of it, she reaches her left hand over to grab the piano, stands up, and says, "I'm gon' show you how to walk." The song bursts into an up-tempo tune, and Willie Mae Thornton, with all the unknown pain moving through her body, gets up and does what looks like a mellow but enthusiastic pop lock solo. Hands flailing with precision, she proudly moves with the muumuu across the stage. The bottom line is that "Hound Dog" gives her strength. The audience witnesses Willie Mae's magical resistance; "Hound Dog" is not a song punctuated by defeat.

Willie Mae exits the stage, but upon her return she's wearing a full three-piece suit with a towel around her neck and a cowboy hat. Contrary to Cheatham and Spörke's observations, I do not feel tension between Willie Mae and Sippie Wallace. Like her banter with Aretha, Willie Mae encourages Sippie to "go head and sing" whenever Sippie pauses between lines and lyrics. For the remainder of the song, Willie Mae and Sippie exchange verses, not like they are insulting each other's men and mothers, but like they are role-playing. Something fascinating also occurs when Sippie assumes the position of a scorned lover "who ain't gonna take it no more," and Willie Mae responds as though she's the lover being scorned: "I'm walking out the back door," she says. Sippie, in her dazzling red, sequined dress, and Willie Mae, in her handsome gray suit, are engaged in a playful lovers' quarrel. The back and forth is a crucial queering of the blues — or better yet, it highlights the queer elements in the blues. Son House famously said that the blues ain't nothing but the feelings that come from problems between a man and a woman. The stage play between Sippie and Willie Mae (reminiscent of vaudeville drag performances) honors all the blueswomen before them who decided to love each other publicly, either romantically or maternally and sexually or spiritually, in ways that "authentic" bluesmen have never been allowed. As if knowing this was one of her last performances, Willie Mae shows up and shows out and embraces everyone on stage in the process.

Nineteen eighty-four was culturally rich and socially heavy. That year, I heard my father call my mother from across the house with sad urgency to share that Marvin Gaye had been killed by his father. Black LA folk took Marvin's death personally, constantly talking about how he died "right over there off of Gramercy." In New York, Jean-Michel Basquiat held an exhibition at the Mary Boone Gallery in Soho and was figuring out the sound of his work while shaping underground club culture, all the while cautious about the art world's clamor around his name. Few of us knew what to make of Michael Jackson's 1984 visit to the White House. He dedicated the proceeds from "Beat It" to an anti–drunk driving campaign, which felt like an endorsement of the Reagan administration's "Just Say No" propaganda. With Nancy Reagan leading the political charge, the campaign justified aggressive War on Drugs policies that ruptured families and communities. Def Jam Records was established in 1984, and *The Cosby Show* made its debut.

Without a doubt, Prince's sixth studio album, *Purple Rain*, and the feature-length film of the same title solidified his emergence as a force to be reckoned with. Tina Turner rose up from the ashes of a weighted history to procure a place in white stadium rock history as a solo artist. So not just a comeback from Ike, but a reclamation of her rightful place as a Black southern originator. Her 1984 Grammy Award–winning album *Private Dancer*, with its hit single "What's Love Got to Do with It," was nothing short of a brilliant reinvention rooted in Nutbush resilience and Buddhist ritual. Herbie Hancock and Grandmixer DST's "Rockit," one of the few Black videos that circulated on MTV's openly racist programming (we love David Bowie for standing up for Black music), not only snatched a Grammy but stood out as one of the first visual representations of Black musical cross-pollination centered around rap music and the culture it spawned.

Music and cultural critic Nelson George pointed out that by 1984 there was "a tremendous rise in the availability of crack and the appearance of dozens of 'rock houses.'" As a nine-year-old in 1984, I saw how the influx of these rock houses accelerated the mass incarceration of hundreds of thousands of friends and families across the country. My mother, cousins, aunts, and uncles included. In 1984, the CDC reported 4,918 AIDS cases, and of those, 2,221 of the patients died. Some who succumbed to the disease between 1984 and 1990 were cast members of Jenny Livingston's film *Paris Is Burning* — Dorian Corey, Willi Ninja, and Angie Xtravaganza. Say their names.

In July of 1984, I can imagine a sharply dressed-in-a-suit Willie Mae making her way through her last tour. In my mind, she struts onto the stage and sits down on the chair placed next to the mic. Even while sitting, she's tall. Willie Mae crosses her right leg over her left, pauses, looks at the crowd, and receives the love, shouts, and cheers before taking a drag from her cigarette. A minute has passed and still she allows the applause to carry her over. What she's telling folk with her silence is that they are in the presence of Black cool. Willie Mae Thornton is cool as fuck. The kind of cool that allows her to keep a cigarette between her fingers with one hand as she pulls her harmonica out of her jacket pocket with the other. The song she sings is "Ball 'n' Chain," and, consistent with how she has performed it for over thirty years, she announces, "This is a song I wrote, and I'm gonna sing it in my own way." She's carrying an air of righteous stubbornness — unshakable pride. That night, the message was clear. Willie Mae Thornton told the people, employing Black cool as the face of the message, that she owned every song she sang, regardless of whether she wrote it. She owned her unique performances, her gender-nonconforming fashion choices, her gin, her height, her blues, her worldly gospel.

The truth is, Willie Mae was in pain through most of the early '80s, and her touring schedule was brutal. It's no wonder the alcoholism intensified following the car accident. The line between addiction and pain management was blurry. On July 25, 1984, a few days after the show I created in my mind, Willie Mae Thornton — in Los Angeles, the place where I took my first breath — took her very last. When I think about this moment, my hope is that Willie Mae spent her last year deeply satisfied by how she changed the face of music — how she bent the notion of a blueswoman into different shapes. Assuming she did, I don't want to dwell on the details of her death. I'd rather use that energy finding the unmarked grave, lifting up her body of work, and giving her the peace after this life she deserves.

Muddy Waters died a year before Willie Mae, and Sippie Wallace, two years after. Aretha's father, the Reverend

C. L. Franklin, and Willie Mae died two days apart. There are ghosts throughout these pages—their stories, wins, aspirations, and losses have haunted my pen. But the ghost of Willie Mae is one we must protect from scarcity-driven stories that hide her accomplishments and keep her in the loop of unnecessary pity and shame. Her experience in the American music industry is a cautionary tale, yes, but much more interesting is the fact that she crossed borders, had a child whom we must commit to remembering, taught grown men how to play their instruments, and fought the forces (people and systems) that attempted to exploit her.

Willie Mae collaborated with the greats because she was a great. These people lived the blues, and the blues are complex in that they offer what Clyde Woods refers to as a "tradition of explanation," a way through the hard-to-anticipate twists and turns in the collective world of Black people in the afterlife of slavery. Willie Mae outlived Janis Joplin and Elvis Presley, both of whom were tortured by some of the same demons that hovered above Willie Mae, but she stayed and played hard until she was ready to leave. She lived several full lives and for decades found new parts of herself in front of live audiences, both in the States and across the Atlantic. She worked a lot so that she could eat, but most of all she modeled a kind of misery resistance that makes it clear that the blues, in addition to being an epistemological intervention, is also a technology of survival. Willie Mae Thornton knew who she was, and she left a map for us to find her again and again.

EPILOGUE

I began writing *Why Willie Mae Thornton Matters* on December 11, 2020, on what would have been her ninety-third birthday. The pandemic raged into the New Year while I watched America implode on January 6, 2021, from Westerpark, a small neighborhood in Amsterdam, the Netherlands. I was no "Stranger in the Village," like James Baldwin when writing his first book in the Swiss Alps. I'd visited Amsterdam over the course of six years and grown closer, with every visit, to its daily rhythm. The stillness of the place, created in part by the pandemic's national curfew and early winter nights, allowed me to quiet my mind enough to listen. What spoke to me was an amazing combination of voices from both Willie Mae's journey and both of our maternal lineages.

My walk through Willie Mae's life inspired fierce curiosity about women in my family whose spirits I'd never had the pleasure to meet. This book is for Willie Mae's grandmother Eliza and her mother, Mattie. It's for my great-grandmother Helen, my grandmother Mattie, and my mother, Vadis. It's for my youngest sister, Vikki, and my older sister, Franchelle, and the twin nieces, Logan and LaShawn, she gave birth to on my thirtieth birthday. It's for my sister's first daughter, Faith, an Aries. And for her daughter, my first great-niece, Kaini.

Their names, because of the ritualized scholarship this story called on me to perform, are ones I now call on a regular basis. All the women who showed up for me — the way spirits do — were, like Willie Mae and myself, wander-lusters and skilled survivors. The book itself reflects my movement through the world and was written between the UK, California, Ohio, Italy, Massachusetts, and different cities in the Netherlands. Willie Mae performed, recorded, or had a bottle of whiskey (like I had a joint), in every single one of those places. I'm proud to say that Willie Mae and I share similar paths — mothering each other on the page, under the needle, and through speaker boxes in the process.

ACKNOWLEDGMENTS

Like Greg Tate, dream hampton is a patternmaster, and it was he who introduced me to dream. She introduced me to the legendary music critic Evelyn McDonald, who had reached out to her to write an essay for the anthology *Women Who Rock: Bessie to Beyoncé, Girl Groups to Riot Grrrl* (2018), and dream (producing multiple films/documentaries/series at the time) passed the opportunity on to me. For that anthology, I wrote my first two published music essays — one on Santigold and the other on Björk. Evelyn understood the contrasts between the artists and the place where their works intersected. I was honored to receive an email from Evelyn after working together on *Women Who Rock*, inviting me to submit a proposal for Music Matters, a new book series she was editing. She suggested I write about Prince a year after his passing in 2016. Unsurprisingly, there was a slew of new books on several aspects of his career. Prince studies had become a legitimate though informal discipline, even if on the margins of academia. More importantly, I had already become more familiar with Willie Mae Thornton by that time. When I suggested a book on her instead, knowing there had only been one biography and very little footage of her live performances throughout her forty-year career,

Evelyn responded enthusiastically, and here we are. This is the origin story of how *Why Willie Mae Thornton Matters* became my love project. I am also incredibly grateful for the unwavering loyalty and thoughtfulness of Dr. Chandra Nirmala Frank, who, through this process, transitioned from my romantic partner to my forever family. Our history of writing and thinking together changed what I understand of what it means to be in community. Thank you for eating, drinking, and walking across continents with me for seven years. Writing retreats in LA, Amsterdam, London, and Cincinnati. International Locals and kitchen poets, together. What a blessing to watch you snatch up your PhD and then push me to apply for my own at the same institution soon after. Goldsmiths, University of London meets *Mississippi Masala*. Love you and Sir Bentley Diego deeply. In June 2020, I moved to Amsterdam and became part of a diasporic writing community, including intimate Zoom room sessions during the pandemic lockdown with Simone Zeefuik, Marly Pierre-Louis, Daphnia Misiedjan, Noleca Anderson Radway, and Taylor J. Lemelle. Thank you for making this book possible. And to my chosen family, Ira and Ayra (Kip Republic), who kept me working so I could ease my way into the Netherlands, as I wrote with Willie Mae, thank you. Thank you, VaNatta Ford and Satchie Ford, for the soulfulness you brought to my life in Massachusetts. Thank you for seeing my work and creating a space for me as the Distinguished Sterling Brown Visiting Professor at Williams College. Willie Mae was right there with me. Thank you, Terisa Siagatonu, for offering me the gift of poetry, which put a creative fire under this experimental biography. Thank you for believing in my words and for always finding the pulse in the pieces I share. You're smart and sharp, attentive, generous, and watery — with a mean pen. I love you. To the London people who checked for me and helped me land. Thank you, Faiza Bashe, Jenn Nkiru, Zezi, and the dopest Somali astrologist from Kilburn, Hodan Omar Elmi. Thank you to my lifelong friend, who kept candles on my altars and on my desks throughout the writing process, Saladin Henderson (TheB.U.Exp.). Thank you to the women musicians and music writers who inspire me: Elissa Blount Moorhead, Fredara Mareva Hadley, Zandria Robinson, Maureen Mahon, Karen Good Marable, Imani Wilson, Danielle Amir Jackson, Tricia Rose, Daphne Duval Harrison, Holiday Harmony, Joi Gilliam, Barby Asante, Tamar-Kali, Imani Uzuri, and Anisia Uzeyman. Thank you to the soulful academics and creative scholars who model other ways of moving on the page: Saidiya Hartman, Joy James, Stuart Hall, Louis Chude Sokei, Hazel Carby, Alexis Pauline Gumbs, Kevin Quashie, Angela Davis, Michael A. Gonzales, Pierre Bennu, Treva Lindsey, Sarah Haley, and Saul Williams. Thank you to the curators who teach me how to see differently: Tiffany Barber, Rambisayi Marufu, Rashida Bumbray, Desiree Mwalimu, Makeba Dixon-Hill, Maori Karmael Holmes, Rhea Combs, Sandra Jackson-Dumont, and Savannah Wood. Thank you to Khanyisile Mbongwa for Black Atlantic love in the key of care and cure. Thank you to the women DJs who move the crowd in all the ways: DJ Reborn, DJ Rimarkable, Sabine Blaizin, DJ Monday Blue, Novena Carmel, Wyldflower, and Cyndi Handson. Thank you to the people who believed in my work and created opportunities for me to grow it: J. Bob Alotta, Novella Ford, Kimberly Juanita Brown, Skye Larkspur, Nydia Swaby, Victoria Adukwei Bulley, Zella Palmer,

Amal Alhaag, and Zoe Dille. Thank you to the folks at Stanford's Institute for Diversity of the Arts. Thank you to Adam Banks and A-Lan Holt for welcoming me and for keeping me in the family as a Visiting Artist. Thank you to Michael Spörke, whose book on Willie Mae inspired and informed much of this work. Thank you, Casey Kittrell, LeVon Williams, Niela Orr, and Kim Mack for being the first people to lay eyes on the Willie Mae manuscript. Your collective suggestions felt like a sharpening of my spirit as a writer in general. Thank you to my family and to the youngest person related to me, my great-niece, Kaini.

SOURCES AND REFERENCES

"The AIDS Epidemic in the United States, 1981–Early 1990s." Centers for Disease Control, n.d. https://www.cdc.gov/museum/online/story-of-cdc/aids/index.html.

Alabama, and John G. Aikin. *A Digest of the Laws of the State of Alabama; Containing All the Statutes of a Public and General Nature, in Force at the Close of the Session of the General Assembly, in January, 1833; To Which Are Prefixed, the Declaration of Independence, the Constitution of the United States, the Act to Enable the People of Alabama to Form a Constitution and State Government, &C., and the Constitution of the State of Alabama. With an Appendix, and a Copious Index, and Also a Supplement Containing the Public Acts for the Years 1833, 1834 and 1835.* Tuscaloosa, AL: D. Woodruff, 1836.

Alberta Hunter: My Castle's Rockin'. Directed by Stuart A. Goldman. Pottsdown, PA: MVD Entertainment Group, 1988.

Bailey, Moya. *Misogynoir Transformed: Black Women's Digital Resistance.* New York: New York University Press, 2021.

Baldwin, James. "The Discovery of What it Means to Be an American." In *Nobody Knows My Name: More Notes of a Native Son*, 17–23. New York: Dell, 1961.

Banks, Adam. *Digital Griots: African American Rhetoric in a Multimedia Age.* Carbondale: Southern Illinois University Press, 2011.

Baraka, Amiri. *Blues People: Negro Music in White America.* New York: Harper Perennial, 1999.

Beserra, Fidel. "Top 10 Blues Harmonica Players." *Blues Rock Review*, April 22, 2021. https://bluesrockreview.com/2021/04/top-10-blues-harmonica-players.html.

"Big Mama Thornton 1970." Television performance with the Buddy Guy Blues Band, aired on WGBH on the program *Mixed Bag*. YouTube video, 00:06:02. https://youtu.be/IJlBo5KJ3b4.

"'Big Mama' Thornton and the Holding Company." *Fifth Estate*, June 26-July 9, 1969. https://www.fifthestate.org/archive/82-june-26-july-9-1969/big-mama-thornton-and-the-holding-company/.

"Blues Is a Woman Newport Jazz Festival. 1980." Organized by Rosetta Reitz at Avery Fisher Hall. YouTube video, 02:06:15. https://www.youtube.com/watch?v=opkyoIht_9c.

Bradley, Lloyd. *Bass Culture: When Reggae Was King.* London: Penguin, 2001.

Sources and References

"BRC Manifesto." Black Rock Coalition, n.d. https://blackrockcoalition.org
/mission/manifesto/.

Campbell, Bebe Moore. *Your Blues Ain't Like Mine*. New York: Ballantine, 1992.

Carby, Hazel V. *Cultures in Babylon: Black Britain and African America*. London: Verso, 1999.

Chude-Sokei, Louis. *Dr. Satan's Echo Chamber*. Cape Town: Chimurenga, 2012.

Cohen, Aaron. *Aretha Franklin's "Amazing Grace."* London: Continuum, 2011.

Cole, Teju. "Black Body: Rereading James Baldwin's 'Stranger in the Village.'" *New Yorker*, August 19, 2014. https://www.newyorker.com/books/page
-turner/black-body-re-reading-james-baldwins-stranger-village.

Cone, James H. *The Spirituals and the Blues: An Interpretation*. Ossining, NY: Orbis, 1992.

Davis, Angela. *Blues Legacies and Black Feminism: Gertrude "Ma" Rainey, Bessie Smith, and Billie Holiday*. New York: Vintage, 1999.

Denise, Lynnée. "House Music Is Back: Let's Remember Its Roots." *Harper's Bazaar*, June 30, 2022. https://www.harpersbazaar.com/culture/art-books
-music/a40473664/house-music-is-back-lets-remember-its-roots/.

Du Bois, W. E. B. *The Souls of Black Folk*. Chicago: A. C. McClurg & Co., 1903.

Duncan, Amy. "Female Blues Singers Who Weren't So Blue." *Christian Science Monitor*, March 27, 1984. https://rosettatribute.weebly.com/uploads
/2/6/0/4/26042866/christian_science_monitor.pdf.

Echols, Alice. *Scars of Sweet Paradise: The Life and Times of Janis Joplin*. New York: Henry Holt, 2000.

Elvis Presley: The Searcher. Directed by Thom Zimny. New York: HBO Documentary Films, 2019.

Frank, Alex. "Rap Pioneer Roxanne Shanté Finally Gets Her Moment." *Pitchfork*, March 19, 2018. https://pitchfork.com/thepitch/rap-pioneer
-roxanne-shante-finally-gets-her-moment/.

Free Show Tonite. Directed by Paul Wagner and Steven Zeitlin. Raleigh: North Carolina Department of Cultural Resources, 1983.

Friday. Directed by Felix Gary Gray. Los Angeles: New Line Cinema, 1995.

George, Nelson. *Post-Soul Nation: The Explosive, Contradictory, Triumphant, and Tragic 1980s as Experienced by African Americans*. New York: Penguin, 2005.

Gilmore, Ruth Wilson. *Golden Gulag: Prisons, Surplus, Crisis, and Opposition in Globalizing California*. Berkeley: University of California Press, 2007.

Gumbs, Alexis Pauline. *Revolutionary Mothering: Love on the Front Lines*. Oakland: PM Press, 2016.

Gunsmoke Blues: Muddy Waters, Big Mama Thornton, Big Joe Turner, George "Harmonica" Smith. Directed by Michael Burlingame. Dallas: TopCat Records, 2004.

Gussow, Adam. *Whose Blues? Facing Up to Race and the Future of the Music*. Chapel Hill: University of North Carolina Press, 2020.

Sources and References

Halberstam, Jack. "Queer Voices and Musical Genders." In *Oh Boy! Masculinities and Popular Music*, edited by Freya Jarman-Ivens, 183–96. New York: Routledge, 2007.

Haley, Sarah. *No Mercy Here: Gender, Punishment, and the Making of Jim Crow Modernity*. Chapel Hill: University of North Carolina Press, 2019.

Harrison, Daphne Duval. *Black Pearls: Blues Queens of the 1920s*. New Brunswick, NJ: Rutgers University Press, 1988.

Hartman, Saidiya. *Wayward Lives, Beautiful Experiments: Intimate Histories of Social Upheaval*. New York: W. W. Norton, 2019.

Hartman, Saidiya. Lose Your Mother: A Journey along the Atlantic Slave Route. New York: Farrar, Straus and Giroux, 2008.

Henriques, Julian. *Sonic Bodies: Reggae Sound Systems, Performance Techniques, and Ways of Knowing*. London: Continuum, 2011.

hooks, bell. *Feminism Is for Everybody: Passionate Politics*. Boston: South End Press, 2000.

Hunter, Marcus Anthony, and Zandria F. Robinson. *Chocolate Cities: The Black Map of American Life*. Berkeley: University of California Press, 2018.

James, Etta, and David Ritz. Rage to Survive: The Etta James Story. 2nd ed. Cambridge, MA: Da Capo Press, 2003.

James, Joy. "'New Bones' Abolitionism, Communism, and Captive Maternals." *Verso Books* (blog), June 4, 2021. https://www.versobooks.com/blogs/5095-new-bones-abolitionism-communism-and-captive-maternals.

Janis. Directed by Howard Alk. Universal City, CA: Universal Pictures, 1974.

Janis: Little Girl Blue Documentary. Directed by Amy Berg. Venice, CA: Disarming Films, 2015.

Jones, Gayl. *Corregidora*. Boston: Beacon, 1987.

Jones, LeRoi [Amiri Baraka]. *Black Music*. 1967. Reprint, Cambridge, MA: Da Capo Press, 1997.

Kauppila, Paul. "From Memphis to Kingston: An Investigation into the Origin of Jamaican Ska." *Social and Economic Studies* 55, nos. 1/2 (2006): 75–91.

Kay, Jackie. *Bessie Smith: A Poet's Biography of a Blues Legend*. New York: Vintage, 2021.

Lipsitz, George. *Midnight at the Barrelhouse: The Johnny Otis Story*. Minneapolis: University of Minnesota Press, 2013.

"Lithofayne Pridgon on Jimi Hendrix (1973)." Excerpt from the 1973 documentary *Jimi Hendrix*. YouTube video, 00:04:20. https://youtu.be/VhJz58XxTjg.

"Little Richard Interview with Bill Boggs." Aired on *Midday with Bill Boggs* television program. YouTube video, 00:34:55. https://youtu.be/B2CqEzy3iv4.

Lorde, Audre. *Zami: A New Spelling of My Name*. Watertown, MA: Persephone Press, 1982.

Sources and References

Lordi, Emily J. *The Meaning of Soul: Black Music and Resilience since the 1960s*. Durham, NC: Duke University Press, 2020.

Mahalia Jackson: The Power and the Glory; The Life and Music of the World's Greatest Gospel Singer. Directed by Jeff Scheftel. Santa Monica, CA: Xenon Pictures, 1997.

Mahon, Maureen. *Black Diamond Queens: African American Women and Rock and Roll*. Durham, NC: Duke University Press, 2020.

Makeba, Miriam, and James Hall. *Makeba: My Story*. New York: Plume, 1989.

Martin, Douglas. "Rosetta Reitz, Champion of Jazz Women, Dies at 84." *New York Times*, November 14, 2008. https://www.nytimes.com/2008/11/15/arts/music/15reitz.html.

Morrison, Toni. *Playing in the Dark: Whiteness and the Literary Imagination*. New York: Vintage, 1993.

Neal, Mark Anthony. *What the Music Said: Black Popular Music and Black Public Culture*. New York: Routledge, 1998.

Nina Simone: Live at Montreux 1976. Directed by Jean Bovon. Montreux: Montreux Jazz Festival, 2005.

"Otis Blackwell on Letterman, January 10, 1984." Interview and performance aired on *Late Nite with David Letterman*. YouTube video, 00:09:57. https://youtu.be/AgzzJ-eV8JY.

"Ray Charles — Interview with Bob Costas." Interview aired on NBC in 1999. YouTube video, 00:16:11. https://youtu.be/0vDP72531FA.

Ritz, David, Jerry Leiber, and Mike Stoller. *Hound Dog: The Leiber and Stoller Autobiography*. London: Omnibus Press, 2010.

Roxanne Roxanne. Directed by Michael Larnell. New York: i am OTHER, 2017.

"Roxanne Shante on Biopic, KRS One Beef, Baby Father Abuse (Full Interview)." Interview posted on *VladTV* on April 9, 2018. YouTube video, 00:59:37. https://youtu.be/utNtvaVR-YQ.

The Russell City Blues: Stories and Music of a Lost East Bay Community. Oakland: Past and Present Media, 2010. See https://www.youtube.com/watch?v=ADo9-YAflaQ&t=25s for more information about this event.

"Sam Phillips the Man Who Invented Rock & Roll (Part 1)." Documentary aired on A&E Biography Channel UK. YouTube video, https://youtu.be/tYcadYXsTyM.

Sawyer, Wendy. "The Gender Divide: Tracking Women's State Prison Growth." Prison Policy Initiative report, January 9, 2018. https://www.prisonpolicy.org/reports/women_overtime.html.

Serwer, Jesse. "Independence Rap: Pop Art Records' Hustle Put Philly on the Hip-Hop Map." *Wax Poetics*, 2009. http://jesse-serwer.com/pop-art-records.

"Sippie Wallace, Big Mama Thornton, Jeannie Cheatham: Three Generations of the Blues." Television program aired on PBS, directed by Crown

Sources and References

Propeller. YouTube video, 00:57:42. https://youtu.be/O-fd3cNc8tE.

Smitherman, Geneva. *Talkin and Testifyin*. Detroit: Wayne State University Press, 1986.

Spillers, Hortense. *Black, White, and in Color: Essays on American Literature and Culture*. Chicago: University of Chicago Press, 2003.

Spörke, Michael. *Big Mama Thornton*. Jefferson, NC: McFarland, 2014.

Steptoe, Tyina. "Big Mama Thornton, Little Richard, and the Queer Roots of Rock 'n' Roll." *American Quarterly* 70, no. 1 (2018): 55–77.

Szatmary, David. *Rockin' in Time: A Social History of Rock-and-Roll*. Englewood Cliffs, NJ: Prentice-Hall, 1987.

Swavola, Elizabeth, Kristine Riley, and Ram Subramanian. *Overlooked: Women and Jails in an Era of Reform*. New York: Vera Institute of Justice, 2016.

Thornton, Big Mama. "Big Mama Talks with Chris Strachwitz." Bonus track on the CD reissue of Big Mama Thornton, *In Europe*. El Cerrito, CA: Arhoolie Records, 2005.

Walker, Alice. "Acclaimed Author Alice Walker on Her Book, 'The Same River Twice: Honoring the Difficult." Interview with Charlie Rose, January 29, 1996. Video, 00:15:47. https://charlierose.com/videos/3843.

Walker, Alice. *You Can't Keep a Good Woman Down*. New York: Amistad, 2003.

White, Charles. *The Life and Times of Little Richard*. London: Omnibus Press, 2003.

Wild Women Don't Have the Blues. Directed by Christine Dall. San Francisco: California Newsreel, 2018.

"Willie Dixon, Sunnyland Slim and Big Mama Thornton Discuss Their Careers in the Blues and Describe Some of Their Songs." Radio interview by Studs Terkel. Audio, 00:30:59. https://studsterkel.wfmt.com/programs/willie -dixon-sunnyland-slim-and-big-mama-thornton-discuss-their-careers -blues-and-describe.

Woods, Clyde. *Development Arrested: The Blues and Plantation Power in the Mississippi Delta*. London: Verso, 2017.